The 7th Drummer

Sam—
Thank you so much
for all your help.
Check out the Acknowledgements.
also page 170.
~ [illegible]

For my parents, and for every person who taught me to love music.

Prologue

Once upon a time, in a land far, far away, there lived a mighty King. The land he ruled stretched far and wide, full of things like cows and horses and wheat, because that's what kingdoms were usually filled with. But, the kingdom was also filled with people, which is typically the problem Kings have with their kingdoms. The people had a tendency to storm the doors of the castle as the King was having public hearings, which usually led to shouting matches that could be heard in the neighboring kingdom of Mira. The King called a meeting to solve this problem (the Queen couldn't focus her needle point over the sound of the wailing and had threatened to leave the King as a result.) The deliberations lasted all day and night. When the sun was high over the castle for the second time, one exasperated courtier blurted out, "Why don't you just let the people in already?"

After the few shocked silent moments passed, the King said, "That's not a bad idea." The advisors rushed to tell him the peasants would sooner tear him apart than sit like proper gentle people, but the King refused to budge from the idea of inviting some of the public in to show his sympathy towards the plight of the common man.

Many days later, they finally had the plan. The Plan to restore peace and silence to the kingdom of Bora.

They would invite twelve orphans to live with them, almost identical in looks, with green eyes and brown hair and all under the age of sixteen. After a separate wing of the castle was constructed and completed, a servant was sent to collect them. The boys were brought back to the palace and soon became bored stiff. As many people will tell you, Royal court wasn't all that fun, not since the wailing peasants were sent home.

To entertain them, the Courtier taught them to create rhythms on drums, and they all took to it immediately. After all, anything would beat hearing the trials over farm animals and land waivers that were heard in the throne room at that time.

The orphans took to drumming, and so was born the tradition of the twelve drummers.

Chapter One

"Alright, alright!" Master Linus shouts at us from the floor above, "That is enough practice for today. My wrists are hurting too badly. You are all dismissed, after you clean up." Tired, I stick my drum sticks into the pouch on the side of my drum, wiping the top off with a rag. Light shines through the windows, bathing the stone Drum room in stained-glass glory, almost like a cathedral for tired boys and rhythmic patterns.

The heavy wooden door on the open floor above us closes with a loud sound, like a breath being exhaled, signaling that Master Linus has left us all behind. But when I look up, there's Georgia, the king's daughter, staring at us. Her large purple eyes scan the drummers, watching us clean up, her dark hair falling in tendrils over the lip of the wall. Her chin rests on her crossed arms as her face shines in the golden light of the windows. But then, the oldest drummer here, Conner, walks up the long, twisting flight of stairs to meet her, and I hear them talking over the shuddering noise of everyone else cleaning up.

"Hey, Georgie," he says, teasingly, "Run out on the ladies in waiting?"

"Yes," she says, "and don't call me Georgie." Their voices echo throughout the hollow building, bouncing off the walls so all of us drummers below can listen in without fear of being caught eavesdropping.

"What was it this time?"

"They tried to make me wear a ball gown." She crosses her arms over her chest.

"Frilly?"

"Pink."

"Oh." He leans against the stone wall that serves as a railing, watching us below. Mounting the stairs myself, I tuck a book under my arm and pull my jacket tighter about me. The stone gets cold this time of year. The door to the drum room is set deep in the stone bricked wall, a few paces from the staircase, heavy and oak paneled, but the hinges don't squeak when I open it. We take good care of what we've been given; what little we all actually have.

The heavy oak door opens to a lonely hall, lacking in stained glass, but with a view out both sides to make up for it. Since this is the drum wing of the castle, my room is yet six steps out the door and down the hall, a giant stone semi-circle that houses six beds and little else. The one desk that is nestled in the corner, however, does squeak, and when I get there, I sweep aside the loose papers and open my book. I'm the first one here, not a surprise. That's how it ought be. The five other guys that share this room are probably out, partying with the pages. Celebrating Conner's birthday- his sixteenth birthday. Tomorrow, he ages out; he'll leave the castle gates with twelve gold pieces, sixty silver pieces, and ninety bronze pieces rattling in a canvas pouch, to hopefully find some place decent to stay before the sun goes down.

Then, three hours later, a boy who's exactly twelve, will show up at the gates, led by Master Linus. As the new arrival, he will take the place and number of Connor. He will be the new Seventh Drummer in a court of twelve.

Shivering, I break my thoughts from the possibilities and stoke the fire, to chase the chill from the room. Kneeling with my back to the fire, I tilt my book so the light catches the words, like ink-storytellers. I sigh, content.

****

Oh, it was awful. They wanted to meet me in the ballroom. That was fine. It was when I saw the giant pink ball gown in the middle of the floor that I ran to refuge with the drummers. I thought the dress was on a form, but I was wrong. They had starched the fabric so much it stood by itself, which was unnatural in every way.

I ran out the door without saying a word to Mother or whoever else she brought in to turn me into a lady. I know so many secret passageways and short cuts in the castle, even my most trusted friends (mostly pages and drummers) can't keep up. This time, I slid down the banister, into the library, out the library window, climbed the trellis. I unlatched the plate-glass window to the hallway, and landed in the Drum Wing, right outside the two-story practice room. The sound of the drums pound through the thick stone walls, adding a pulsing rhythm to the atmosphere. But then they stop, and the doors fly open, despite the thick wood that insulates some of the noise from the outside world. Master Linus comes rushing out, rubbing his wrists and saying something about getting in a carriage. I've always found him as a sort of odd, mousy man.

I pry open the heavy door and watch the guys clean up, resting on the stone wall. The drummers set their drums on the floor, carefully detaching the straps to hang them on the curved wall under the arching stained-glass windows. They move slowly, talking to each other as they wipe down their drums and lay them against the walls. The twelve drummers stick their music parchments into leather music rolls, slinging them on their backs and mounting the stairs. First one up is Conner, who stops and talks to me, like normal. Like I'm actually supposed to be here, not the social anomaly that I am.

The small talk he tries to make is frustrating, and pointless. "You're leaving," I say, tapping my fingers on the stone wall. "You're leaving." My voice bounces off the wall, the syllables a short imitation of the drumming that was just pounding through the walls of the castle.

We're alone now, the rest of the drummers having left through the practice hall. "Yes, I'm leaving," he says, taking my hand and leading me down into the circular room below. "I must leave tomorrow- I turn sixteen."

I sit on the rug fashioned to look like a drum that lies in the center of the room. "Surely you can appeal to someone, to stay here." I pluck at a loose thread on the hem of my dress, nervously. He sits down next to me, not facing me but angled just enough.

"Sadly," he begins, "I can't. I'm planning to head to the coast, along the lower eastern half. Port Seaglass. To begin work as a fisherman." I say nothing, just look at him, his hair and eyes to match the rest of the drummers. As is law. As is tradition.

The words of his plans hit the floor between us, dead. "You know," I finally say, "You know that I'm going to miss you." I raise my eyes to his.

"I know," he says, "And I promise I'll write. Maybe you could come visit for holiday."

I stand up and stretch, though it hasn't been long. "Or maybe you could just not leave."

He smiles, "That's not really an option." But we both know neither of our suggestions were much of an offer anyway.

Connor stands up as well, just as the doors open. When the doors to the Drum Room open, you always hear them before you see who stands there. The hinges don't creak, but there is a sucking sound, like an in-drawn breath. High above us stands another drummer with a page behind him. The drummer is spinning drumsticks between his fingers and the page stands with his hands resting on the hilt of the sword tied at his waist.

"Come on, Connor," he says, "You're going to miss your own going away party!"

“Very well, very well,” Connor says, making his way to the stairs.

From the top of the walkway, Connor leans over the stone barrier wall. Something white flashes in his hands, an envelope folded out of new parchment. Dropping it, it falls faster than I expect it to, but still I pluck it out of the air. I pull out a necklace, a crystal ball on a gold chain. It’s fraught with imperfections, cracks and glimmers that catch the golden light and throws it, but that’s what gives it character.

“Really?” I ask, looking up at the friend I’m about to lose.

“Thought of you,” he says with a playful smirk, heading out the door with the other drummer and page.

****

Chapter Two

The sun shines in my eyes, golden rays of light, and I blink, tears fuzzing up the corners of my vision. Conner left three hours ago, and I have been waiting outside ever since. We all have. It's not everyday that there's a new drummer, ready to be trained. The sun again. I shift a little to the left, so the tree blocks the brunt of the sun, and focus back on the book propped in my lap, the rays making the ink glimmer in the light and illuminating every speck that hangs in the air. In my right hand is an apple; in the left is propped my chin.

Cries are heard across the square, both from the other boys and the gates as they swing open. Standing on the other side is a boy, hands thrust deep into the pockets of his brown trousers, eyes downcast. I wish I could say he looked extraordinary, but he doesn't. He has the same brown hair and green eyes the rest of us do, except that his eyes are a little greener and his hair is a tiny bit darker than mine. But nothing extraordinary. No, you can't be extraordinary and be a drummer.

Master Linus steps into the middle of the circle. "This is Janson Tucker," he announces, his voice carrying and bouncing off stone castle wall, "He is now the 7th Drummer." With that, he is done, and he walks forward toward the castle, leaving the drummer behind, standing confused.

I look at the other eleven drummers spread out on the ground about me. It's a little warmer today, a little bluer, than it has been in the past weeks. I hear the pages battle-training in the courtyard, high pitched metal on metal and a shriek of rage. But not a word comes from the drummers as we stand and gaze at the newest arrival. The newest addition to the corp. Our newest charge.

As I dust my knees off and stand up, I catch the purple-eyed Princess Georgia looking down from the tower, examining us from above. Not that that's unusual in the slightest.

Wandering through the halls of the castle, I go to the library and grab another adventure book, one I've read many times before, from the worn, wooden shelves. Its light green spine tries to break away, but I won't let it. Carrying it gently, like a baby, I take it back to my room. As I walk down the barren, stone halls, I hear the sound of drums. Not skilled, but weak. The beats are slow, long, and spaced out. The snare drum, with its classic fast rattle. Ch, ch, ch.

Turning to the right, just before I reach the practice room, I step inside my own dorm. Setting the fragile book on the desk, I sit on my bed to think. Or, reminisce, rather. The green eyes of the drummer haunt me, the look of… well, not terror, but uncomfort. The look of- the look of an outsider.

The chair creaks as I lean back in it. I remember coming here, years ago. I was scared, a little orphan taken off the streets, like many of the drummers are. I knew nothing about music, less about drums, and I was… well, scared. It was all frightening to my little, twelve-year-old self. But that's what it's like to be transplanted. You're taken from the comfort of routine to this new place, full of people you're so desperate to please, learning a new trade that hardly anyone knows.

Shaking the memories from my head, I reach over and take the book in my hands, diving into the fast-paced adventure.

All too soon, though, the doors squeak open and the other drummers, a few dripping with water, come in. One of the wet ones, Seamus, takes his shirt off and hangs it from one of the hooks above the fireplace. Hanlon hangs his socks from a different peg, leaving a pool of glassy water on the stone hearth.

There's a knock on the door. Seamus pauses stripping off his own socks to twist the brass handle. Standing there is a very scrawny and a very sunburnt Janson Tucker.

"Hey," Hanlon says, brushing a lock of wet hair from his eyes. "So, you're the new guy." It's a statement, not a question.

"Yes?" It was a question, not a statement.

"I'm Seamus," Seamus says. He points to the bed in the middle of the semi-circle. "That's your bed."

Then the guys resume changing out of their wet clothes, murmuring about numbers being called for the Creek Game, a cruel thing that involved a twelve-sided dice and fully clothed boys being tossed into a freezing October creek when their number was called.

Janson sits on the edge of his bed, plucking at the loose skin around his nails. Something to do when you don't know what to do. He stares at his feet stuck in brand new leather shoes, not broken in quite yet, the blisters that rim the tops of his feet where the leather rubbed unsocked skin. When the other drummers seemed to be more concerned with slapping each other with wet socks and suspenders, I lean over to the trembling seventh drummer.

"They're not as bad as they seem," I say, slowly turning the page in my book.

Nervously, he nods, still looking at his shoes.

Later, when the lamps are put out, and the only sound is the fireplace crackling and the snores of the Drummers, I hear the muffled sobs of the scared Seventh Drummer.

****

I wake with the sun streaming through the windows of my tower to a knock at the door.

"Princess Georgia?"

"Yes," I say, trying to pull the sleepy tones out of my voice, "What do you need?"

"Your father requested you get ready for your dance lesson."

"Very well," I call back, "I'll be down in a minute."

"Miss?"

"Yes?" I say to the door.

"Your mother sent a gown as well… Let me just come in, I'll…"

"No," I say quickly, "I can quite well dress myself, thank you." Though I can't hear it, I feel the sigh of the disapproving lady through the door.

Listening carefully, I hear the handmaiden's footsteps down the stone stairs, and a presence has left. I pull myself out of bed and slip on a white, linen underdress. Over that, I pull on a lighter-weight blue dancing gown.

I don't know why Mother keeps getting gowns sent up here; she knows as well as anyone else that I don't like to wear dresses. Annoyed, I look at the mirror affixed between the wide windows of my room. Tucking my dark curls up and pinning them into place with more pins, I pull a few pieces of hair out. They spiral down around my forehead in lazy loops, impossible to ignore. Almost as if my hair and I agree when it comes to annoying Mother. Lord knows it doesn't work the way I want it any time else.

When I open the door, yet another pink gown waits, tucked in a neat, gold trimmed box. I look down at it; it's almost the same as the rest of the gowns that already reside in my closet. Stepping around the box, I walk down the staircase that winds around the square tower. My room is at the top, so it's a long way to the ground floor. They started building this tower when my oldest brother was born, and just added another floor whenever another child was added, one room to each floor. I have five brothers, and alas, I am the only girl. And the youngest. Which leaves me no purpose except to be worried over by my Mother, protected by my brothers, and left to marry.

I walk down the desolate hallway and into the ballroom. It's only ever used when Mother tries to give me horrid dance lessons. Standing in the middle of the floor is Mother, Mandy, the dance instructor, and a Page.

"Hello, dear," says my mother as I approach, "This is Tristan, your dance partner."

Tristan bows and I curtsy, because that's what is expected of me. "Madam," Tristan says. I say nothing, another silent dagger toward my mother. My mother sits down in a chair off to the side, picking a piece of needlepoint up off the seat.

"Now, Georgia, Tristan, positions, please." Tristan places his hand on my waist and I lay my hand on his shoulder. This page is muscular, no doubt from the fighting, but I can't, cannot, think of that now. It's now, in this quiet, mind-distracting moment where I notice that the strings are missing.

Usually Mother or Mandy calls in a string quartet, or perhaps a pianist, to play music to dance to. Not today. Today Mandy strikes her hands together, loud claps that ring throughout the empty hall like swordstrikes.

Clap. Clap. Clap. Rhythmic. Beats. That. Pound.

"One, two, three. One, two, three. *One, two, three!"* Mandy's counting gets louder and more forceful the more my feet lag behind. And I kind of feel bad. I can dance, contrary to what my mother thinks, and with every step on Tristan's toes I feel worse.

"Ok, ok, ok," Mandy says, "Stop. Just stop. No, Georgia, this is how you execute that turn." She turns her feet inwards and plants her heel, an awkward turn for a woman wearing long skirts. But, anything to avoid stepping on the feet of the gentleman. She sighs deeply once more. "If you cannot dance, then why bother to be a lady?"

"I don't know. I'd rather learn to drum than learn to dance," I murmur under my breath. I watch Tristan's mouth twist into a sidelong grin, but he returns to his dancing posture and we regain dancing position. I glance over at my mother, who is absorbed in her needlepoint. How can needlepoint be so engrossing?

Because my mother isn't paying attention, and because I can dance, I decide to waltz perfectly for the next run. "One, two, three," Mandy counts, and I can hear the chance in her voice when I stop stepping on toes and tripping over my skirts. I execute that turn perfectly, and this one too. Even this one, which is a difficult spiral within itself, regardless of skirts. "One, two, three?" Mandy's voice slips further, softer, and more unsure than ever.

"Faster," I say to Tristan, and we begin to pick up speed. We twirl faster and faster; my skirts begin to twirl outward. Mandy stops counting all together, and just watches us spin.

"Fox trot," I say, counting a few measures in soft breath to get us started, we transition from waltz to fox trot. We dance fox trot for a few moments.

"Do you know quick step?" Tristan asks.

"Of course," I say, grinning, "How would a lady not?"

We twirl round and kick our feet high with the quick step. My skirts swirl through the air, the lace underskirt flipping and turning around my ankles with every kick. After a few bars of the quick step to silence, we stop. Panting a bit, Tristan bows deep and I curtsy.

I turn and see Mandy's face is red and irate. "You knew how to do all that, and you made me look like a fool!?" She turns on her heel and storms out. Mother looks up at Mandy's shouting, startled at seeing the newest instructor rush out the door.

Standing up, Mother goes and follows a still-shouting Mandy into the hallway.

There's a moment that hangs in the air like a silk scarf.

Mother returns, pale and slightly angered. "Mandy has quit… again," she says, "and won't come back like last time." In a huff, she leaves the room, her heels clicking against the floor angrily.

"Thanks for that," I say to Tristan, "I needed to get rid of her. She was worse this time than the last!" He grins and puts his hands on his hips, still breathing hard.

"Any time," he says, "Any time." He smiles and walks away, too. Leaving me alone once more.

****

All the drummers stand in a somewhat lopsided circle, drums slung over shoulders with broad leather straps. In the center is the bent Master Linus, clapping his hands and marching around his drum, which is on a stand.

"Now, for the Call to Arms," he says, waving his hands in the air, "The Call to Arms, boy." This was directed to Janson, who was flipping through pages of parchment wildly and dropping his drum sticks on the ground. “Janson, Janson, stop,” Master Linus says to the confused boy, “It’s this one. This piece of parchment.” He stoops over and picks up a yellowed piece of music off the floor. He hands it to the boy, who places it on the wooden stand in front of him.

“Begin.” A pause, another pause. Then beats. Long, short, ladadiddle, short, long, rest... Slow, in unison, except the beginner, who is still managing to mess up. Each missed hit, each missed rest, each missed rim shot stands out like a sore thumb. And there are a lot of them.

“Again. Begin,” Master Linus says. A pause, another pause. We start the short run over again, but this time, there are fewer mistakes.

“Ok,” Master Linus says, “Better. Much better. You are all dismissed.” All the Drummers slouch and shrug the straps off shoulders. They carry the drums and set them on the stands around the rim of the room. They hang the broad leather straps on the wall, and tuck unused music parchment into music rolls. They slowly trickle up the stairs.

Except for me. And Janson.

We stand in the middle of the room, our drums still slung out, the ancient single stand still set up.

It's my day to tutor. Whenever there is a new drummer, all the older drummers take turns in tutoring the new guy. This way, he gets better quicker. "Ok, Janson," I say after all the drummers have left the room and sound no longer rattles through the windowpanes, sound no longer trapped in the stone. "Here we are." I pick the drum up off the ground where I had let it rest, lifting the strap over my head so the snare fits comfortably in front of me.

"What am I doing wrong?" Janson says, sitting on the ground, "Why can't I get it right? You guys all seem like you know what you're doing."

"That's because we do," I say matter-of-factly, "But we've all been here a lot longer than you."

"When will I get it?"

"There are some songs I still don't know. We don't really play those much."

"Oh." Janson looks down at his music, somberly. Not that he's smiled much in the past few days or anything.

He focuses on his music, slowly hitting the skin drumhead and trying to decode the music set upon the stand in front of him.

"Quarter rest."

"What?" He looks at me, then back at his music.

I point to his music. "You missed the quarter rest."

"Oh," he says. "I'll restart." I nod, and he restarts. Going very slowly, he proceeds to play the Call to Arms very well.

"That was very good," I say, "That's great, really. Here. Take the drum to your room and keep practicing. It's too big, too cold in here." The circular Drum Room is large and echoey, which doesn't help with timing, but besides that, it has no fireplace. Whoever built this room didn't do a very good job thinking things through. It's an impressive room, but a horror to heat.

Moulded underneath the stairs, right where they start to curve too much, is a bookshelf. The shelves are laden with odds and ends particular to drumming, but none of them used much. From the shelf second to the floor, I pick up a circular block of wood covered in soft, pale doeskin.

"Here," I say, walking back to the center of the room and handing the block to Janson.

"What is it?" he asks, examining it, the soft edges covering hard wood.

"It's a drum pad. You fit it to the drum like this." I fit the drum pad over the head of the drum, so that when Janson hits the drum, he hits the doeskin covered wood and not the skin head.

"Now, bang on it. Play a run of notes," I instruct Janson. He plays a set of notes, fast and rapid, and sporadic. But all the sound that is made is a dull, hollow thwack. Not even the rattle of the snares.

"Hmm," I say, smiling. "See? The magic of drum pads. Now, I'm going to go to the room and read some."

"Arlan," Janson says, making eye contact for the first time. "You're forever reading. Why don't you ever spend time with the other drummers?"

"I just don't care for them," I say, mounting the stairs. Janson follows me up the stone incline, trailing one or two steps behind.

As we reach the door, I open the heavy oak, holding the edge so Janson can pass through first. Standing right in the doorway is Princess Georgia, her purple eyes glowing against her dark hair.

"Princess," I say, nodding my head and moving past into the long and empty hall.

"Princess," Janson echoes, the one bit of formality he managed to pick up. But, since he is new and naive, he asks, "What are you doing at this end of the castle? Why are you not sewing tapestry or some other womanly thing?"

"Janson," I whisper, standing back. He can't be under my charge and disregarding the Princess.

"No, it's quite all right," Princess Georgia says, the last rays of sunlight twinkling in her eyes, "I don't like that sort of thing. In fact, I spend a lot of time with the Drummers."

"Does the King not mind?" Janson asks, setting his drumsticks into the pouch attached to the side of the drum.

"Not at all," she says, "It's the Queen I need to be concerned about. But, it was nice meeting you, Janson, Arlan." With that mysterious meeting, she goes over to the glass window and unlatches the hook that was keeping glass against wood. Pulling her skirts up a few inches, she lifts herself onto the sill and out into the dusk. I stick my head out the window and watch her climb the last few feet of gable and run off, toward the stables. She gathers her skirts round her legs, scooping up the lace in her arms. There must be a game of Ball tonight.

"Janson," I say, "Go practice later. Here, I will show you the chief past time."

Janson nods, mouth still agape, setting his drum on his bed in our room. He follows me out the window, down the wooden slatted gable, and into the night.

****

After that rather awkward meeting with the drummers, I jump out the window in the cooling dusk. As I fall through the air before catching hold on the gable, there is a gasp, and I can't help the surge of…pride…in my chest. But, I have done this many times, so the catch onto the white slatted lattice is merely a trick to impress newcomers. I climb down the trellis and through several fields. There is a game of ball tonight, and I intend to play, and prove my resilience.

Ball. The favorite past time of the boys, played in stolen nights and in the hayloft of the stables. It's a dangerous game, which is why no adults must find out. It's also why my brothers wouldn't let me play if they knew. But they aren't here now, and they can't stop me.

I stop by the red berried cranberry bush and fish out Connor's Ball gear. I take off my dress, revealing the breeches and white shirt that I put on earlier. I tie the guards on and tie my dark tresses up with a doeskin string, so they won't get in the way.

When my dress has been hidden in the bush and everything is quiet, I approach the stables.

"Aye," says a voice, "Who goes there?" A boy about my age leans out a door cut in the wall far above my head. He holds out a lit lantern and squints down at me.

"Princess Georgia," I say, tilting my face up toward him.

"Aye, Princess," he says, leaning back in. I walk through the crack in the doors that open with a wave of the gate-keeper's hand. Despite the inky blueness coating the outside, the stables are full of light pouring from lanterns with the blinders pulled off and discarded. Sitting on the loft, with feet kicked over the sides, are the boys. My younger three brothers, several drummers, and a couple of pages are all astonished at my presence, mouths agape. They're all wearing the same gear as I, chest pads and back pads. Forearm pads and shin pads. Soft leather, stuffed with fabric scraps make up large rectangles. These are then tied on with leather straps, to hold them securely. I pull out a pair of fingerless canvas gloves, the last piece of the gear, meant to protect from rope burn, I affix them to the pads on my forearms, fitting my fingers through the threading finger holes.

I walk down the aisle in the middle of the stables, past both sides of the loft, chin up, daring anyone to stop me. I climb up the ladder at the other end of the aisle and onto the left side of the loft. Here, there is a red stripe painted along the edge of the loft. A blue stripe is painted on the side of the loft across from us. I sit down next to Tristan, the page I danced with earlier.

"I didn't know you played ball," he says.

"First time playing," I reply, "But I've watched for years."

He adjusts his wrist guard. "Playing is always a very different thing than watching."

I nod.

Slipping in through the crack in the doors comes two drummers, and they join the crowd, sitting on the dirt floor of the aisle and looking up. The audience is composed of kitchen servants, ladies in waiting, along with a couple of drummers.

"Ready, boys?" The gatekeeper boy says. He pauses, "And princess." The gatekeeper-boy closes the wall door and latches it shut before sitting down across from me.

Another boy, a page I don't know well, stands up. "You all know the rules. Swing with the ropes. Hit your target on the opponent's side. No pushing people off the loft… at least, just don't get caught." He reaches into his pocket, pulling out two jars of paint- blue and red.

Tossing the jar to a page on our side, he unscrews the lid. Dipping his fingers in, he draws a long blue line down his nose and to his chin. Then he draws a horizontal line across his face, quartering it. He passes the jar to the boy on his left, who dips into the paint and quarters his face. Both jars pass along opposite sides, until the jar reaches me.

I dip my fingers into the rusty red paint and draw the line down my nose. The paint is wet on my skin; cool in the night air that leaks through the doors. I draw the horizontal line, before passing the paint to the page on the other side of me.

It reaches the end of the line of players, where the jars are sealed up, their lids pressed hard against the glass. There is a kitchen maid below us in the aisle, her skirts dancing around her ankles as she holds her hands up to catch the jars when they drop down. With a small clink, the jars get arranged upon on a table that's been set up on that end. Tacked to the wall down there is a large piece of parchment, she sticks her fingers in each jar and smears a wipe of color on each side. Each team's scorecard.

"Ready?" says the page next to me. But he doesn't get a chance to finish.

"This is the ball," says the page who told the rules. He pulls a small, fist sized ball from his pocket. It glows. I mean, the opaque rubber glows in the dull lamplight, an eerie green color. An unnerving, unnatural palor leaks from the yellowed ball, giving off enough light to shine but not enough to illuminate anything. The rubber was mixed with mountain powder when it was still hot, the specks forever embedded within it, forever cursed to leak light for midnight Ball games, like now.

Mountain powder- another reason we don't want the adults to know. It's cob-coled goods: bought off the black market. It's only produced in the Glass Mountains, the east side of Mira, and prized for its many, illegal, properties.

The rustle of fabric fills the air around me, and I shake my head clear of the thoughts, tucking a strand of hair in a hairpin, moments before the games begin.

"Set, go!" shouts the page, tossing the ball into the air. It hits the ceiling, and comes plummeting down, just in time to be caught by a red player, swinging by on a rope.

"Pass here!" A red team boy comes swinging across, one arm outstretched. The game goes on all around me.

Backing up three steps, I run swiftly and grab onto the rope. I feel the coarse hemp catch onto my gloves, pulling them until they don't slide down any further. Momentum carries me across the pass, dropping me safely on the other side.
"Georgia!" someone cries, but then the ball is coming toward me. But I don't react, except that somehow, I do. The ball is in my hand. Turning around, I roll the rubber across knuckles before tossing it at the target. It hits the blue circle with a gentle thump before landing on the slightly angled loft boards. The glowing rubber ball starts rolling toward the edge of the split loft, before dropping neatly into the crowd below.

Silence, or as close as you can get in a crowded barn.

Some of the boys are shocked, not aware that I had arrived. Others are swinging back over sides and resetting for round two. The girl on the floor dips a quill into a jar of ink, making a small mark underneath the smear of red paint. One point for us. Nineteen to go. Short rounds make short games.

We reset. Again, the ball is tossed up, and again, it's taken by a red player. But, a blue team player throws his shoulder into the red player with the ball. The red player is thrust sideways, stumbling to catch balance on the uneven boards. Falling over the edge, he grabs onto a rope, too low, and swings across. His body hits the ledge, and he grapples for purchase on the stable walls. The poor player stumbles to catch footing, having lost the rope, scrabbling on the wall. If he fell, mayhap he's hurt, but he's definitely out of the game. His feet catch purchase on the top of an open stall door, leaving him sprawled out on the edge of the Red side.

Meanwhile, Blue scored, and those that cheer for them do, their voices ringing up towards the heavens.

****

I have seen a lot of games of Ball since I first came, many years ago, but that one was one of the best, if not the most memorable. It's not every day that the Princess Georgia plays the game, swinging across the divide, over the audience below, long dark tresses flying behind her.

Janson walks up to me as we walk out the door into the cool night. "How was your first game of Ball?" I ask him.

"It was quite well," he says, yawning across the wildflower fields. The moon is low in the sky, but tomorrow is our day off. Master Linus says that if we are run hard every day, we will come to resent drumming. I say, as long as I have food to eat, clothes to wear, and books to read, I will make do with what I can find.

Walking in silence, side by side with Janson, I overhear the pages talking with Princess Georgia behind us. "You did great," one says to her, a loud, barrel chested older Page. "You didn't even fall off. The first time I played, I broke my collarbone, crashed into the wall while I swung from a rope. Had to tell people that I fell off my horse." She laughs.

"Yes, well," she says, "I don't really have an excuse for a broken collarbone."

"What are you doing tomorrow?" another one asks, taking his arm guards off and hanging them from his belt.

"Probably sneaking out and going into Jade City," she says, untying her gloves and holding them between her teeth while she unties her chest guard.

“You should. That’s what we were planning, as well,” the first one says.

“Aye? I will, then,” she says, taking the white gloves out of her mouth. But, then we reach the separate Page’s quarters, and we must cross the courtyard and climb the lattice.

“Goodnight, Princess,” I say, climbing the lattice with my back turned.

“Goodnight,” she replies, “Hope I didn’t frighten you, Janson, when I jumped out the window.”

He smiles, grabbing onto the lattice to begin to climb. “Not at all,” he says impishly. “Good night.”

She nods, smiles at him, and turns around. With long strides, she disappears into the darkness, away from the circle of buttery lamp light.

Leaning out the window, I pull Janson into the hallway, gangly arms first. With a little more practice, he’ll get the hang of climbing in through the window. “What was that about?” Janson asks, his face alight in the moon coming in through the open window, “The princess playing ball?”

“She’s tougher than she looks,” I say, “Not that anyone gives her credit for it. Now go practice.”

“Alright,” Janson says.

Our dorm room is dark, and cool against our shoulders, the embers in the fire burnt down low. Here, we are expected to kindle our own coals, and not have a maid do them for us, unlike the other parts of the castle. Kneeling at the hearth, I crack a couple of sticks and start the fire up again. We're the first ones back to the lonely room.

The pale sounds of Janson pulling out the drum pad from the corner where it was stored resonate throughout the room, just like his slow, unsure strokes do. I grab one of the navy woolen blankets from someone's bed, and sit by the fire, reading against the reddish- orange light of the fire.

******

Chapter Three

I walk through the crowded streets of Jade City, my head covered with a flowered straw bonnet that also hides my face. My dark hair is brushed out, not braided up, falling natural, with loose curls near the bottom. I rather prefer it like this- braiding takes too much time and pain to be worth doing every day, in my opinion. And to disregard Mother. To her, having long hair and keeping it braided up is what makes a lady. Which seems to contradict itself, but I don't get a say in the matter. Except for the marvelous days like these, where there is excitement in the air and a gentle breeze to blow through the straw bonnet affixed to my head.

We walk about the stalls, looking through booths and listening to vendors hawking their wares. We run our hands over the smooth cloths dyed brilliant colors, page through books bound in colored leather, gaze at pastries set out on a counter to cool. One of the drummers walks past a necklace vendor, running his hands through the hanging strings. They collide together with musical clinks, reminiscent of a wind chime in autumn. "Hey!" shouts the vendor master, "Get out of here or buy something!"

The drummer walks away from the vendor indignantly, joining me in line for the pastry vendor. "Oh, good morrow, Janson," I say, taking a handkerchief from my sleeve. "Two pecan pastries, please," I tell the girl running the stand. Her long hair streams down her back in tight ringlets the color of the pastries under the window. She takes my handkerchief and wraps the warm pastries in them, handing them back.

"Natalie," someone calls from within, and the girl turns, mussing with other pastries and breads on the counter, arranging them under warm, damp kerchiefs to rise in the sunlight

"C'mon," I say to Janson, "Let's find somewhere to eat."

Next to the market is a city square, nearly untouched by the market neighboring it. Almost no one is around the barren square, and set in the center is an old marble fountain. It's old and worn, and it's been as such as long as I can remember. Janson and I sit on the edge of the stone, eating our pecan pastries.

"Georgia," says Janson, mouth full, "Why do you prefer drummers, instead of your ladies in waiting?"

"They're so boring," I say, taking a bite, savoring the salt in the caramel and the toast of the pecans. "All they do is talk about who they think is handsome, and sew and gossip. They're nothing but predictable."

"Makes sense," he says, dipping his hands into the fountain water to wash the sticky caramel off. "So, besides playing ball, what do you do? There's not much talk about you, at least not in Jasmine Jewel, where I used to live."

I reach into the sleeves of my white dress, drawing from the left one a book of poems, and from the right one, the New Testament. "I sit in the wildflower fields and read these."

I offer them to Janson, who takes them and flips through the pages, glancing at the sticky thumbprints and tea drop stains. "Interesting. I would never have said you were the poetic type. Adventure, maybe, but never poetry."

Taking the book back, I stand up. "Well, I guess I'm full of surprises." I tuck the books back into their sleeves and fold up the handkerchief and tuck that into my sleeve as well.

"Is that where you're from?" I ask, adjusting my full skirts and sitting back down. "Jasmine Jewel?"

He nods, "It's a small town, on the banks of a river fed lake. There are jasmine flowers growing everywhere, even along the roads, and the air smells fresh, like… like water. It's the kind of place where kind-hearted merchants settle down and raise families. Where the girls have long, braided hair and blue eyes."

"Not like here."

"Not like here. It was small, almost everyone knew everyone, and the local boys would throw each other into the lake." He smiles, but it fades quickly. "It's full of memories. More sad than sweet." Janson props his arms on his knees, laying his head in his hands.

"More sad than sweet?" I probe, "How so?"

He seems to consider this. "It didn't really have a set orphanage, like other cities have. The orphans lived on the streets, or built forts in the woods. They only came out when there was something to do, something to say, someone to talk to. But, when the page came with the news that they were looking for a new drummer, I had to take the chance. I wanted to do something… and get out of that town." His voice is quiet now, low and calm.

"Get out of that town?" I ask, resting my elbows on my knees and leaning forward. "You're quite mysterious, you know."

"I know," he says, his forehead creasing with lines, "I see you want to know my secrets, aye?"

I don't respond.

"My parents were killed in that town. Fire. I… couldn't stay." His voice is so quiet now, I have to tilt my head to listen.

I nod, lowering my eyes, "I'm sorry."

****

My plan was to stay in bed and read late in the morning, under the warm wool blanket. But, of course, that didn't happen.

"Wake up!" The other drummers toss me out of bed, like a ragdoll, and onto the cold stone floor. "Wake up!"

"Why?" I ask from the ground.

"We're going into the city, yeah?" asks Hanlon, pulling a pair of worn grey suspenders up over his shoulders.

"I guess," I say, sitting up and fishing my shoes out from under my bed. Maybe I can pick up a new journal while I'm out.

All around the market, there were plenty of wares to be had, but none that I needed. Reams of parchment, lengths of fabric, clothes. Foods. And the aisles between the stalls were full of people, going to buy something special for a someone, or getting must-needs for the upcoming season.

The only book vendor in the whole market this week was tucked towards the center. The walls were closed off with oil paper walls to keep out the cold breeze that blew by every once in a while, the door covered with a length of wide ribbed boning cloth. The shadow-colored boning cloth fell closed behind me as I stepped into the vendor stall, bathed in a yellow glow from the oil-paper.

Oh, books. I breath in the wonderful woody smell of paper, the fantastic tinge of the words printed upon them. So many titles crowd tables, so many I haven't read. So many I wish I had time and pocket money to read, and yet know I never will. They lay on the wooden stall tables, bathed in the same oiled golden glow as the rest of the stand, but when the light fell upon the books, it changed them. They were no longer mere paper and ink, but now portals and escape hatches built into a convenient, pocket-sized square.

Nestled in the warm corner of the stall, the vendor master sat, leaning over an open book splayed in his lap. I lean a little over his shoulder, to see what he was reading. "That's a good one," I say aloud.

"Is it, now?" he asks looking up, "Been on my shelf for years, and I had never picked it afore now. Aye, and I'm halfway through it." He closes the book on a scrap piece of paper, scribbled with numbers and merchant's calculations. "Are you looking for anything in particular?"

"Just a journal," I say, picking up a simple vinegar-paper journal, bound in tanned leather. "How much is it?"

"Three bronze." At least the price is good, and low for the journal. Us drummers aren't given that much spending money as it is. I fish the coins from the pouch in my pocket, and hand them to the old vendor master. He takes the journal and wraps it up, in butcher paper and twine.

"Thank you, sir," I say, turning to go.

"Wait, boy," the vendor master calls out. I turn. He holds up the book that he was reading. "If you like this book, you'd be well do read some O'Connor," he says, sitting down on his squat, three legged stool once more.

"Yes," I say, nodding, "Good day to you."

"And to you," he says, hunching over the book once more.

I pull the fabric flap open and step out into the cool breeze. The wind draws ripples through my hair, and draws lines on the surface of the water in the fountain in the square, and balancing on the side is Janson and Princess Georgia, neither saying a word to the other.

I walk over to them and sit next to Janson on the cold marble fountain. “Have you got a pencil?” I ask Princess Georgia, who reaches into her sleeve and pulls out a little piece of charcoal wrapped in linen strips. I take it from her fingers and start writing in my little vinegar paper journal, pushing the closing strap to the side.

“Arlan.”

I look up, “Hmm?”

“Where did you come from?” Janson asks, looking at me, but the princess has pulled her book of poems from her sleeve and is committing one to memory.

“I lived in a little town in the northwest, called Jasmine Jewel,” I say, returning to my journal.

“With the fresh air and blue-eyed girls?” Princess Georgia asks, looking up from her book, enchanted.

“Yes.”

“Sounds lovely,” the Princess says, smiling down at the book of prose nestled in her hands.

“It was,” Janson says.

“You too?” I ask, looking over the top of my journal.

"Aye," he says, looking down at his hands. I go back to writing. A drummer calls the Princess over, holding a swath of fabric up. She stands up, making a big ordeal about getting her skirts in order and muttering about what she wouldn't give for a pair of britches.

"Janson," I say, "Have you been fishing?"

"A' course," he says, looking at me curiously, "All the time."

"I'm done with the city," I say, looking at the chubby cheeked marble cherub atop the fountain, worn so with age it is hard to tell what it once was. "Want to go to the creek and fish?"

"Sure," he says, quietly, "It's culture shock, coming from Jasmine Jewel to here, you know?"

"Aye," I say, "It'll get better." And it does, though it never quite goes away.

We walk down to the creek, a little ways from the road that leads up to the castle. The Castle sits atop a small hill, at the base lies the city, and a well-cared for cobbled road connects the two. It winds up the small side of the hill, so the path is straighter, though it still bends. The creek lies where the straight part turns for the first time, where the land to the side of the hill is flatter and the pools are deeper. These deep pools are the point of many a fishing day and Creek Games.

Leaves crunch underfoot as we walk through the brush. Dried leaves fall to the ground around us as we knock into the small saplings, a simple rain falls from them. Near a boulder that barely sticks out of the ground, there's a false tree, constructed by the eldest princes many years ago, and is now used to store fishing poles. The door swings open, revealing the six or seven poles there, along with fake baits. The bottom shelves are full of dusty jars, used for catching bugs, now long forgotten, empty. There are few boys who still use it.

"I've been down here afore, but I didn't know this was here," Janson says, examining the contents of the fake tree, and seeing how the wooden plaster ware was molded to look like the other trees. He runs his fingers over the molded, rosin wood and examines it against the other trees.

"Aye," I say, "You wouldn't see this, unless it's been pointed out." I pull out my rod and a spare for Janson, handing it to him.

"Thanks," he says. He pulls on the string, it loops outward like a spider web- it's a little sticky, but as much you'd expect from it sitting in a fake tree for several years. I grab a couple fake baits, a few lures, and lead Janson to my secret fishing spot. A tree stands above the water, its roots sticking out and making a seat- just wide enough for two.

"This is the best place to fish down here," I say, pulling the string out of my pole and dropping the line in the water below us. Underneath our feet, dangling inches above the water, the current of the creek cut deep into the sides and the bottom. The muddy floor of the creek is far below the water line, and filled with brush, too. It is there that the fish like to gather, so have I learned. I stretch my toes into the water below, feeling the slight current flow around my skin. They leave little v's, water filling in the space our toes left in the stream.

"I used to go fishing all the time in Jasmine Jewell," Janson says, dropping his spider-web line into the coursing water with mine. "With my parents. We would hike to the river, Mother would pack a lunch, and we'd eat along the shores."

"Sounds lovely," I say. There's a tug on my line, but it's just the current pulling the slack out of the string.

Janson sighs, nodding a bit but he doesn't say anything.

"That's the thing," I say, after a long pause, laden with discomfort. "Every drummer here, everyone that's ever been here and ever will, has no parents. We're all orphans." Janson remains silent, but I can feel that I'm making headway. He needs to open up about his past and trust someone, he's been holding the truth in for too long. Brand new drummers come to the court all the time, messed up and closed off. And, as everyone knows, a stopped bottle will explode eventually.

"How long ago?" I ask, careful to keep my voice steady.

"Two years, next month." His voice is hesitant, drooping at the corners.

"With no one to watch after you? Must've been hard. And a fire? Left with nothing to your name, aye."

Janson nods, his voice starting slow but gaining speed and volume as he talks. "It started one night. Mother tossed me out the window and into the hay. I broke my arm, but then the beams collapsed and the straw caught fire. I ran into the street, screaming and shouting, but by the time the men could come-" He breaks off, shaking his head.

My line jumps, the drop where it meets the water making loops and swirls as it's dragged through the water. Wrapping the line through my fingers, I pull it in. My excitement crescendos, just reaching the crest when the line breaks with a thin popping sound and the fish leaps away. "Aww, got away."

"That always happens to me," Janson says. He looks at me, green eyes large. "If you came from Jasmine Jewell, and so did I, why have I never seen you before?"

"I don't know," I say, "What did your parents do?"

Janson swallows hard, and says his words carefully. It's almost like he could see the words forming in the air in front of him. "They worked for the king."

"Aye, and did a lot of people in Jasmine Jewell."

"I know," he says, "They were…bookkeepers." He pauses, "Retired bookkeepers."

"It's been years, but I think I would've remembered the King's retired bookkeepers," I say, stretching my fishing line out in front of me to tie another bait on. Most of the people in Jasmine Jewell do work for the King, or did afore they retired. They were merchants, or soldiers, or scribes. Most of them retired as well, old and full of stories to tell the children gathered at their knee. But I don't remember any bookkeepers at all. Librarians, there were, but the merchants kept their own numbers. There was no need for bookkeepers. They just didn't settle there.

"Well," Janson says, "That's what they were." He turns his shoulder away from me, like I am a cold winter chill.

"Aye, no need to get up about it," I tell him, gently. "I must be mistaken."

Just then his line jumps, drawing figures in the water over the tumultuous waves. It pulls hard and Janson, though he has a good grip on the rod, can't seem to pull the string out fast enough. He manages to pull the fish far enough in, though, far enough we can see it. It's big, and it may even be the biggest I've ever seen caught here.

"Arlan," he says, leaning back and fighting the fish, the string reeling in and then going back out, "Arlan, can you help?"

I take my shirt off, tying the sleeves closed, pulling the strings taught around the neck and tying them shut with a simple knot. When I dip it in the water, it's easy to scoop the fish up. The water streams out through the fabric, creating a sort of net, white canvas forming to the fish's shape.

We get the fish up on shore, backing away from the edge of the bank so that it doesn't leap to freedom, back in the muddy waters. "Do you want to cook it?" I ask.

"Cook it?" Janson looks around at the quiet forest surrounding us, "Here? Now?"

"Aye," I say, "Here."

"But we've no fire, nor any other means to cook it."

"That hasn't stopped me before," I say. Lying in the mud at my feet are several small rocks, no bigger than the curl of your first finger. I pull two out, wiping the mud off with my fingers, revealing the white below. Janson is watching me with fascination.

"Go on," I say, smiling at his bewilderment, "Skin the fish. I'll have the fire done soon."

With a small nod, he pulls a knife from his belt, slitting the creature down its belly and dumping out the entrails in the water, so the other fish can fatten up. With a quick movement and a single stroke, he cuts off the head, dropping it in the creek as well. Using the needle-sharp tip of the knife, he slices down the meat as he peels off the skin and the scales together, in one piece.

I go about, gathering dry sticks and leaves, setting up a pile on the mud of the forest floor. "For being so young, you can skin a fish just about near as good as the rest of us."

"So I've been told," Janson says, carefully working the rest of the skin free. He stops to watch me as I pull fibers of the wood apart, settling them down on top of my small pile of leaves and sticks. I return to my rocks, striking them together and causing sparks to go everywhere. One or two embers land on the wood, glowing orange and small before causing a fingerling flame. Gently, I blow on the growing spark, and it multiplies, spreading to the rest of the wood. I stick a few more strands of wood fibers in, and the fire grows. Enough to cook a fish in.

"Where'd you learn to do all that?" Janson asks, sawing a flexible greenwood stick off a tree.

"Books," I say. The woods are quiet, and I know Janson doesn't believe me. At least his eyes say so, they're large and green and coated in disbelief. The oil of the fish pops as it cooks over the red orange embers.

"No, really," he says, "Who taught you?"

"I did," I say, "I've read about them in books, and it seemed to work out well for the people on the pages."

"Aye, and so it has for us," Janson says, pulling a bit of the fish off the bones.

Chapter

Four

“Arlan,” They say, bursting through the door.

“Aye?”

“They’re starting the creek game,” Seamus says, “Down at the Deep Hole. You should come.” He crosses the silent room, over to where I’m sitting with my back to the bookshelves.

“No,” I say, “I’m going to stay here.”

“Arlan,” Seamus says, squatting down on the rug next to me. “You never come. You should, it’s a lot of fun. And, we’ve already convinced the new one to come, that shall be fun.”

I shrug. “Seamus,” I say, “I’m not going.”

He lowers his voice, his green eyes flashing. “Arlan, Hanlon went down to the town yesterday, bought a trick dice. Lands seven more than not. Come on, let’s make a fool out of him.”

“No,” I say, “I’ll stay.” And I turn the page to my book.

****

“Georgia,” I hear someone say. I look up from my book of poems, book marked with a flower. Through the glint of the sun, I see it’s Janson.

“Janson,” I say, “What are you here for?”

He sits on the soft dirt, at the base of the rock. My favorite rock, in the middle of the wildflowers in the field, as you approach the castle. His green eyes glint in the sun. “Georgia, are you going to the creek today?”

“What’s today?” I ask, “Are they playing the creek game?”

“The creek game,” he nods, “Aye. I was wondering if you play in that too.”

“Why?”

“Because they’re about to start,” he says, glancing at the sun, it’s level in the sky. “I thought you might want to know.”

I nod, tucking the daisy-flower bookmarked book of poems into my sleeve. My full skirts fall around my ankles as I stand, the lace catching on the flowers around the base of the rock. It's a good day for the Creek Game, the sun is high and bright and warm, and there's no wind to cool you down.

"Is it at the deep hole?" I ask Janson as we walk down the road, toward the bend at the base of the hill.

"Yes, I think so," he says, "They said it was in the usual space."

"Aye, the deep hole," I say, "That's where it always is. It's the only place where you can throw them in and not worry about rocks." He nods, solemnly, as though he knows what the creek game entails. He doesn't, which is why he's playing now. They probably tricked the dice, anyhow.

The banks of the creek are undercut with the fast moving current, and you must be careful not to step too close to the edge, lest you fall in. A premature dunking, one should say.

"Janson," Hanlon greets us as we near the pack, gathered by the river. "Glad you could finally join us."

Arlan nods, solemnly. "The Princess Georgia said she'd tag along with us."

But the other drummers don't care. I've played this game often, more so when I was younger, but enough now. Hanlon gathers us all around. "Twelve?" he asks me. I nod. I'm number twelve, Arlan's number. He's not here, not that he usually shows up at all, anyway. Not since his first day, his trick dice day.

The drummers, cruel as they are, usually have a trick dice for a drummer's first game. The faces come off of the twelve sides, allowing the different sides to be weighted. The weighted face falls down more often than not, and the newest drummer's number up.

The drummer to come before Janson was Ambrose, the skinny Fifth drummer. When they told him the dice was weighted, he threw it into the river. Hanlon dove into the spring waters to get it, cold with the melting snow, but the current carried the small wooden dice downstream, and Hanlon came up sputtering and an unhealthy shade of blue.

"First," Hanlon says, handing the dice to Seamus, the first drummer. He rolls the dice.

Seven.

"Alright, Janson," Seamus says, giving Janson a hefty push over the overhanging edge of the bank. He lands in the water with a great flailing splash, comes up sputtering. But he's a strong swimmer, and he just bobs in the water, and looks at us.

"Come on up, Janson," Hanlon says, laughing at him and offering a hand. When they haul him back up on the bank, he stands there shivering and looking at me, eyes wide with the cold.

"Are you alright?" I ask, and he laughs, good spirited.

"It was a bit shocking," he says, "the cold water. Although, it's been warm this week, I guess it's better than last month."

"Aye," I say. "Roll the dice again!" Seamus laughs, rolling the dice.

Five. Everyone crowds around Ambrose, who just barely has enough time to pull his feet out of his shoes before he hits the water, and comes up with his laces clutched in his hands, laughing.

Before we even have time to pull him out of the water and onto the muddy bank, Seamus rolls once more, and of course it's seven. With a roar, Janson jumps into the water even before the mob can toss him in, laughing all the way till he crashes into the water below.

Seamus leans in closer to me. "Aye, at least this drummer doesn't mind the weight," he laughs, rolling the dice again. Twelve.

"It's you!" he says, looking at me, smile across his face.

"Alright," I say, grinning, peeling off my skirts and running towards the bank, jumping off the edge and diving a perfect swan into the deep hole below. If you hit the water just right, you can glide under the cool, numbing water until the it turns, and climb the roots there.

When I break the water's surface, the drummers are hollering at my dive, jumping and laughing. Oh, how much more entertaining this is than dancing lessons.

Hanlon jumps, shouting, "Roll again! Roll again!" And Seamus does.

Seven.

When we've had enough of throwing each other into the creek, and we've sat in the warm sun to bake us dry in the dying light, we hike back towards the castle, coming in the servant's door, right outside the library. Janson walks alongside me, gazing through the open doors of the rest of the castle.

"What's he doing now?" Janson asks me, standing in the doorway to the library, watching Arlan. He's walking around the rug in haphazard circles, pulling books off shelves at random and sticking them back on with a certain fierceness.

"You know, he resembles a chicken with no head," Janson says again, tilting his head to the side and squinting.

"Aye," I agree, nodding. "But this happens every so often. He finished his last book, and he's trying to size up what book to follow. It's a difficult process, or so he says."

"Ah," muses Arlan. "I'm amazed he hasn't read every book in this library by now."

"This is true," I say, over the aggressive thumping of books on shelves.

Janson grabs my wrist and we walk down towards the Drummer's hall. "Has he always been like that?"

I consider.

"Absorbed in books so much," he clarifies, letting go of my wrist, as though it's an afterthought.

"Aye," I tell him, fiddling with the books tucked in my sleeves. "Ever since he was brought here. He's a few years my senior, I was but this high when he came. But, he still read all the ones he could understand, and quite a few that he couldn't."

"Why?" Janson asks.

I look at him. "Oh, I don't know. When drummers come here, they arrive with a certain amount of… worries."

"Problems, you mean."

"Aye," I say. "Reading was his way of managing."

Janson thinks about this, thinking and twitching his fingers, as though he's playing a piano or something. We're the only ones in the hall, it's empty.

I think about asking him what baggage he's here with but reach the end of the hall all too fast.

"You coming to the game tonight?" I ask him, moving to sit on the edge of the window sill. The window's open, letting in a faint breeze that rushes down the hall and down the way we came. I brush a strand of hair out of my face, but it catches in the wind anyway and goes spiraling back, the dark strands alight in the sun.

"No," Janson says, leaning against the stone wall next to me, "I still need to work on the Call to Arms."

"Really? I'm playing."

"Thanks, though. I came last week."

"Did you?"

"Aye," Jansen says, rubbing a hand over his chin, "We walked back together, remember?"

"Faintly."

"Well, good luck," he says, "You'll need it."

I smile at him. "I'm glad you have so much confidence in me."

He smiles back. "Of course."

I sigh, and drop out the window, backwards, flipping head over and grabbing onto the wooden trellis at the last second. My long silken over-skirt catches on a rung of the worn boards: there's a pull and a rip, a nail ripped it through three inches.

"You're going to hurt yourself, one of these days," Janson warns, leaning out into the night and unhooking the skirt from the trellis. It settles down around me, like the sail of a great ship.

"You sound like my brothers," I say, tipping my head to the side.

I drop the next few feet to the ground and turn into the inky darkness, leaving the sound of Janson laughing far behind.

******

Janson stands in the corner, like he did two weeks ago, after he first arrived.

"Quarter note," I say. He looks up from his drumming, unamused by my joke. I look down again, my journal splayed open across my cotton-laden knees, a wide plain meant for writing. The ink of my quill spills words like fire across the plains. Day to day musings, that such of thing. The ink makes rivers, I have to blow them off before turning the page, lest they smear and marks the pages illegible.

I smile at the compete thought written in ink on the page. But, the ancient clock on the wall is chiming twelve by the time the game is over and the other boys are trickling in. Hanlon, Seamus, and a few others are wiping blue paint off their faces, but Ambrose is washing red paint off with a blue and red stained handkerchief.

"Traitor," Hanlon says, shoving Ambrose into the wall, only playing angry.

"They needed an extra player," Ambrose protests, examining his face in the rain-drop streaked window. It was pouring while they were in the barn, the extra sound and wind, no doubt, adding challenge to the game.

"Now, is that any excuse?" Seamus asks, tossing a wet rag at me. It streams with water as the rag flies through the air into my open palms. I toss it towards the fire. It lands on the stone hearth with a wet slap, a sound akin to a boy crashing into a river, and I know that the fabric will dry stained as well.

"You're forever reading," Hanlon says, unbuttoning his wet suspenders and sticking them in a drawer off to the side. "Don't you ever come out to the game?"

"I did last week," I say, turning the page.

"Last week!" Ambrose scoffs, his hair trailing water. "That was three games ago!"

"I did, I did, and I brought Janson," I say, dipping my pen in the ink pot set on my knee. Hanlon looks at me briefly before taking his shirt off and dropping it in the corner. He jumps into his bed, stretching out and yawning. The other boys start migrating towards their beds, slowly, kicking off socks and pulling off shirts and dropping them on the floor, piling up like haphazard drifts of snow.

"Hey, Janson," Seamus says from under a blanket, "Go stoke the fire." The chore falls to the youngest.

Janson pulls himself out of bed and throws some damps logs onto the fire. They pop up and send sparks all over the hearth, little firebugs. They glow orange for a second, before going out and leaving ash on the grey stone. Janson stands up, wipes his ashy hands on his black trousers, leaving streaks of pale grey.

I turn the page of my journal, finishing off with the date and a signature. I blow on the words, gently, to dry them. When I'm sure they won't smear, I close the cover, tying the whole thing shut with a thin leather cord. My feet hit the cold floor as I walk over to put the vinegar-paper journal and quill set on the desk in the corner.

The room is dim; the only light comes from the fire in the hearth. I slip into bed, underneath the blue, woolen covers. It's warm enough that you don't have to wear a shirt, but the stone around us is cool, and the air slipping through the cracks around the window is colder. Tomorrow, I will fill the cracks with clay, the grey stuff that I find near the creek.

I close my eyes and try to sleep, listening to the ticking of the clock, crackling of the fire, and the gradually slowing breaths of the other drummers.

I sleep soundly, drifting in the grey stuff that makes up drams. But when the heavy chimes of the clock ring four, I wake up. I yawn and roll over, opening my eyes and letting them adjust to the low light. The fire is gone, I can only see by the blue light of the moon, streaming through the window like an uninvited guest. The wool is scratchy as I pull it closer around me, the fibers catching on the skin of my shoulders. Why is it so cold?

My mind shakes off the grip of sleep, and I remember the fire is out. In the hearth. That's why it's so cold in this stone box. I stand up, the flats of my feet against the cold floor. I grab one or two logs from the metal stand and toss them onto the fireplace, onto the metal grille inside. A piece of tinder will do to rekindle the fire. Slowly, flames catch the logs, first the bark and then the heartwood.

There. I stand up and get back in bed.

Something glints in the corner of my eye. Slowly, my mind pieces together that Janson is not in his bed. And the room is so cold because the window is open. And that there is a diamond ring on his pillow. Which means only one thing.

Janson's been kidnapped.

And only one brigand leaves a diamond ring behind when they kidnap someone- Fearless Le Paige.

I light a lamp and open the door to call for help.

Chapter Five

"Tell me what happened, one more time," Master Linus says, sitting on the edge of the bed.

"The clock woke me up. I rekindled the fire. I saw that Janson was missing, saw the ring. I lit a lamp and called you in," I say, pulling the jacket around my shoulders, even though the air is now warm. The window is closed, the fire restarted and blazing. But my skin is still like ice.

"It's classic Le Paige," Clay says, rubbing a hand across his jaw, "I must appeal to the King tomorrow, and get him replaced."

"Replaced?" I say, sitting on the wooden end to the bed, "Replaced? Why don't we find him?"

"It's too futile of an attempt," Master Linus says, opening the door, "You know the stories about Fearless Le Paige. He's long gone, Arlan. I'm sorry."

****

"I'm sorry," I say to Arlan, but he ignores me. He leans farther over the book, shutting me out.

"I know," he murmurs, after a pause, after he realizes he just can't not respond to the king's daughter.

"What are you reading?" I ask him, leaning closer and try to glimpse the title.

"Just a rescue story, Princess," he says, leaning farther over the book, tilting it to shield the title.

"Oh… I see," I say. He's sitting on the floor of the library, surrounded by papers. Scraps of odd parchment, sheets of new. Sitting on top of an open leather journal, a dripping quill leans in a clay inkwell, Arlan's hands are stained with dried ink, a purple tint.

I lean a little closer, over him, and see that he's scrawling notes. On what he's reading, I guess. His loops of writing seem to run into each other, none of them making sense.

Standing, I pick my way over to the poetry shelf and grab up another book of poems; sit on a cushion across the floor from him. The flowery words of prose spill on the page in block printed magic. Most of the poems are in Boran, the language of my country, but quite a few are in Miran, the language of the neighboring country. I can speak fluent Miran, if I think long enough, the only insistence of Mother's that I like. She says it's diplomatic, I'm just glad it doesn't really require frills or fabric of the color pink.

I lean back against the bookshelf, drawing patterns in the dust. They don't clean in here much- when I was little, I asked them not to. The cranky maids and servants kept disassembling the forts me and my brothers made. Not that we make too many anymore.

Arlan stands up, collecting a few papers, but leaving the rest behind with the piles of books stacked on the floor and the quills dripping ink into the wells.

"Where are you going?" I ask, looking up from my book of prose.

"Why do you care so badly?" he says, turning sharply to walk past the heavy wooden door and down the hall. I gather my skirts around me, catching up.

"I won't tell," I try to convince him.

"Doesn't matter," he says, corking the clay jar of ink. He wipes the ink off the tip of the quill, sticking it in his back pocket with black stained fingers. "I'm leaving now, anyway."

"It's dark out," I protest, glancing at the moon through a passing window, "And you're not supposed go gallivanting off wherever you plan, they'll probably catch you."

"I know," he says, yawning. "I'm going to my room, to grab my bag, and then I'm off to find Janson."

"If you'll wait for me, I'll be down in a few minutes. I'll come with you."

Arlan looks at me through hooded eyes. "No, Princess, you must stay here. It's dangerous out there."

"I know it is," I say, making my voice low, "Wait for me."

But there is still a hesitation in his green eyes.

"Look, Arlan," I say, "He's just as much my little brother as he was yours."

I make my eyes meet his, and his drift towards the ceiling, darting between my face and the wooden beams before finally nodding. "I'll meet you in the wildflower fields. Ten minutes, or I'm leaving you behind." He opens the door to the Drummer's dorm, disappearing into the cold darkness.

To my disappointment, though, my excitement quells in my stomach as I mount the stairs up the tower to my room. I half expect one of my older brothers-I'm the youngest- to step out of their rooms and scold me for being out so late. Maybe they might join me in my adventure, depending on the brother. And the mood. And the moon phases. Better to just not get caught.

I stop at the stairs for a moment and ponder what I have gotten myself into. I have never traveled before, although I love to hear the stories of the servants and maids, and where they came from. I've never been allowed, Mother's orders. 'Too dangerous,' she says. But she also says most things I do are dangerous, and I've lived so far.

My room is big and cold and barren. The bed stands sentry in the center of the room, various bureau and closets stand around the edges, most devoid of anything of value… at least to me. The closet closest to my bed is seemingly carved out of a single piece of wood, but if you look closely, you can see the cracks. I reach into the heart of it and pull out a bag, grabbing the stiff leather handle and dragging it out into the middle of the floor. No, this won't work, it's too heavy and too… much. I need a lighter bag. Slipping an underskirt from the drawer, I pull the drawstring at the top tight and tie it off, to make a bag, a makeshift one.

I fill the bag with extra clothes, lighter ones so I can fit more articles in. I take off my silk slippers that I wear around the castle and replace them with a pair of goatskin leather boots. I would wear a hole through the slippers less than a day walking on regular ground, not the stone castle floor, worn smooth over the years. I've already worn through several pairs wearing them outdoors, much to Mother's dismay.

On a second thought, I write a note on a piece of parchment, pinning it to the top of the bag standing in the center of the room. It tells whoever checks my room first that I'm off to rescue Janson from Fearless Le Paige. On the way out the door, I grab my book of poems and Bible off the desk top, spilling papers in the air, but I'm already far down the hall by the time they reach the ground.

****

The wildflower fields smell sweet in the moonlight, their ashen shadows bending in the pale, cold moonlight. I lean against a rock in the middle, a favorite of the Princess, my carpet bag next to me. The leather of my journal is soft between my fingers, even though it's too dark to write, too dark to read. I see the Princess walking toward me, her skirts bright in the night and her red cloak pulled tight around her, reminiscent of the phantoms told in stories spun around campfires by young boys.

"Princess," I say, when she's close enough to hear me. Her face is whitewash in the starless night.

"Drummer," she says back, mocking my formal tone. The princess always did hate how we were made to address her. "Do you know where we are headed?"

"The best I could come up with, from all my searching, is that her hideout is somewhere around the city of Alyak, on Calypso port," I tell her, rising and picking up my bag.

"So, we're off to Alyak, in the dead of night?" she asks, "I assume we're using the main road."

"Of course."

"Adventurous," she says, walking away and through the patches of rough wildflower. She's clearly pleased with this so-called adventure.

I move to catch up with her. It's almost morning when we reach the Jade city, with no carriage or horse to aid us down the long road. The sun hasn't yet peaked over the treetops, but the sky is alight. We move through the heart of the now-quiet city, with its grand cathedrals, intricate shops, and closed open-air markets, not a soul moves. The further down the road we travel, the less kept it becomes, the more we venture into the slums.

Leaning houses are linked together with rope, hung with clothing, wet with dew. Through the open oil-paper windows we hear screaming babies, and as the sun grows higher in the sky, singing. Mothers to crying babes, wives while making breakfast. It's odd, the songs run together, lullabies and morning tunes spin to make the song of the poor. All combined, it's a somber tune.

People are just starting to come out when we reach the edge of town. Women in brightly colored skirts spinning around their ankles step down the streets, to get water from the stream in the woods. Men walk outside, to start stoking street fires that will cook meat later in the day, meat to sell or meat to eat themselves.

I can't help but notice that these people, although they don't have much, are quite happy. Free-er, somehow.

Outside of the city are fields, growing grain, long stalks that bend in the light, spinning a color the shade of Janson's hair. As we walk through it, the sun is warm on my back. It's unusually cold for this time of spring, but I take the thin wool jacket off and, folding it rightly, store it in the bag. A few stalks of grain beckon, and I reach out and grab them from the edge of the field. The husks pull back to reveal the kernels underneath, shining in the dew and shining in the sun. They are my breakfast, a small one. Later, when the sun is higher in the sky, I will pull the cheese from my pack and eat it. The Princess Georgia trails behind me, looking at the sky and the road, at the birds in the fields, and the mice that skitter along with us.

"Princess, have you got any food?" I ask, as we approach the edge of the dire forest.

"No," she says, disappointed, "It was one thing I forgot."

"Well," I say, "We'd better gather grain while we still can. There are no fields in the forest." We slow down for the last few foot falls, filling our arms with grain stalks and holding them preciously. The law says that any man can take grain that is within arm's reach of the road. Being this far out of the city, there is still much to be gathered.

And so, we enter the dire forest with arms full of grain stalks, like poor beggars peddling straw for thatched roofs damaged in the spring storms.

Chapter

Six

The dire forest is full of thieves, and there are trees so thick, they say that words cannot travel through them. The canopy of leaves above us blocks out most light, the path is full of twist and turns. It doubles back on itself many times, but it is only one path. No smaller trails branch off it, though, so as long as you stay on the beaten path, you won't get lost. That's the rules. However, the rules say nothing about getting killed.

We walk through the eerily silent woods, saying no words to each other. The only sounds are our footfalls, but even they don't echo in the padded forest. About midday we come across a group of washerwomen, cleaning clothes at the stream. The stream is only two arm lengths away from the road, I can see it from here. The ladies are laughing and singing, creating rhythm with the beats of the rocks against the wet clothing and spinning words to match it.

I smile to myself. "Quarter rest," I whisper, remembering the days teaching Janson in the drum room.

"Well, good day to you," says the woman closest to me.

"Good day, madam," I reply. Princess Georgia says nothing, instead pulls her cloak farther over her head.

"Travelers, I take it?" the woman says again, "Aye, but mighty young ones, too." She turns her head and sits back on her heels. "Good day, lass," she says to the princess, "Where you off to?"

The princess smiles and bows her head, "Just down the road."

"The sun is hanging low," she says, "If you're heading that way, be as well travel with us. Stay the night." Her companions nod, glancing at the sky briefly before returning to their rocks.

"I did not realize that it was late," I say, "I thought it only to be midday."

"Aye, it is," the woman says, rinsing off the clothing, "But it gets dark far too quickly in the dire forest." She wrings out the shirt, tossing it in the basket between her and the girl next to her.

“Will you spend the night in the forest?” I ask, stepping off the path to help the old washer woman to her feet.

“Will we?” she asks, “No, there’s a town a few miles east of here. But we will, if we must. It’s later than I thought.” The washerwoman’s companions stand up wordlessly, lifting the great baskets of laundry. They slip their arms through the leather straps, using the trees to pull themselves to the path, as if they were walking sticks embedded into the ground. Princess Georgia remains on the path, she never left.

When all the washerwomen are on the path, we start walking. I drift over to the side, next to the cloaked Princess Georgia. The women are chattering, but I can’t make out the words and I’m not sure I care to. In fact, I’m not even sure they’re speaking in plain Boran.

But the oldest one was right, it does get dark early here. We had been walking for less than half an hour when darkness set in, an inky blackness that seems to surround and blanket you. The light that came through the trees slowly faded until there was none at all.

“Here?” suggests a young maiden, setting down her pack of clothes without waiting for a reply. The back of her simple blue shift dress is wet with water that has soaked through the basket, dripping down her skirts and coloring it dark.

“Yes,” the old washerwoman says with a sigh, “here is good.” She sets down her pack and opens the top, but it isn’t full of laundry. It’s full of sticks and ragtag pieces of cloth. She pulls them out, along with some flint, and creates a fire in the middle of the dirt road, another ashen splotch on the packed dirt road.

She sits on the ground next to the fire, and the other washerwomen sit around with her. The one closest to me, with the wet back, takes down her long blonde hair. All the maidens have their hair braided up, crossing their heads in the front, to keep it out of their face. Or I’ve read in books. I don’t know; I don’t have braids.

It’s still day outside the forest, so I’m not tired. The eyelids of the washer-maiden next to me, her eyelids droop, though. Of lack of something better to do, I reach into my pack and pull out my journal. The girl next to me, with the blonde hair, reaches over and snatches the book from my hands, the pages pull at the binding and threatening to come loose. I let go.

“What’s in this?” she says, flipping the pages open and over, leaning over to examine the messy writing.

I grab it back, closing the darkened leather covers and stuff it in my pack. “It’s just my journal.”

“Doesn’t matter,” she says, “I can’t read.” She stares at the flames of the red-orange fire, her fingers playing with a lock of her straw-colored hair. I stare in the fire, the flames spin and twirl like dancers in the darkness. I don't know what to do, I'm usually not the center of attention.

The princess has pulled out her book of poems, committing another to memory. I've seen that this is what she does when she gets bored. None of the washerwomen talk, they just stare at the fire or rebraid their hair, damp from the water on their backs.

My stomach contracts with the familiar pang of hunger, I remember the grain, shoved in our packs, on top of our clothes. I pull out the stalks and start to peel the chaff away from the grain. As I peel, I throw the chaff into the fire, where it pops with moisture before charring and curling up. I make a little pile of grain on the kerchief in front of the fire. We sit in silence. Princess Georgia hands over the stalks she collected, I gather the grain from them.

"Where are you from?" The oldest washer woman asks, her voice an unechoing rumble in the forest. She leans over, pulling out a loaf of lopsided bread and passes it to all the younger women. They break pieces off and pass the loaf to the next girl. When the loaf reaches the straw-haired girl, she passes it over me and to the fiery haired washer-maiden on my other side.

"Jade City," I say, "We're on our way to Alyak." Princess Georgia nods, but keeps her head low.

"Forgive us," The washerwoman says, nodding at the loaf that has reached her once more, "we don't have enough to share." She nods. "Us, we're on our way to return these clothes. We had to pick up some more supplies in Jade City."

"Isn't there much business?" I ask. Jade City is a big place, full of ladies who must need washing.

"No," she says, "They all got their own ladies to do their own washing." Her face crosses with inky, threadbare bitterness.

"Oh," I say. I am quiet, and dreadfully regretting talking at all. I should've kept my mouth shut, like Princess Georgia. The red orange flames illuminate her face, making her purple eyes shine even more.

The blonde lass next to me has turned, so her back is to the fire. The heat is drying the cloth and the strands of hair, wet from the basket also. "Why are you on your way to Alyak? A wedding, mayhap?"

"No," I say quickly, "It's not like that. We're…" But I cannot think of an excuse.

Princess Georgia looks up from her book, lazily, "We're on our way to visit a friend for holiday." She goes back to her book, flipping the page and tilting the book toward the flames.

“How nice,” The oldest washerwoman says, not wanting to converse further.

The rest of the night is spent in silence, on my and the princess’s part. I wonder why the washerwoman was so adamant on us staying with them when we aren’t allowed to eat their food, and they hardly make any effort to talk to us.

I pull the pack around, laying my head on the curl-printed red carpet. It’s rough against my cheek, the pile long and stiff. I pretend the canopy of leaves above us is the sky, and the smoke gathering there from the fire is the clouds, although the sky isn’t usually that shade of moss green and clouds aren’t ash-colored. With that, I drop to sleep, my mind worried with stress and fears.

****

“You there, girl,” says a voice.

I blink the sleep out of my eyes. The man crouching next to me looks kind. His blonde curly hair and ears that stick out a little too much lend to his elvish appearance. I sit up off the ground.

“Yes,” I say. It must be early. It must be very early.

“Did you get robbed? Are you all right?” asks the man, somewhat sympathetically, crouching to my side.

“What?” I stand up and notice that he’s right. Clothes, mixed with ashes, are scattered everywhere on the trail, strewn about. I grab the closest garment, a light blue dress of mine.

I grab Arlan’s arm and pull hard. “What?” he asks, sitting up, his eyes drooping at first and then alert.

“We’ve been robbed,” I say, tossing a bundle of his ashen clothes onto his chest. With a groan and a sigh, Arlan stands up. He looks around, confused, grabbing his carpet bag and beginning to sort through the ash- stained clothes on the ground.

The man stands behind me, silently gathering clothes: dresses, skirts, and petticoats. He gathers into his thin arms.

“Thank you,” I say to him. The man hands me the ashy clothes he was holding, and I stuff them into my makeshift drawstring.

“No problem. Are you sure you’re not hurt?” he asks, putting his hand on my shoulder.

“No, we’re fine,” I tell him, knocking his hand off and stepping back.

He shifts, his green eyes bouncing back and forth, “Just remember you can’t always trust the people you meet on the trail.”

I nod, and stoop to pick up a blouse on the ground. He continues on his way, whistling as he walks.

"Wait," I call, "Sir!"

He half turns, looking over his shoulders.

"Sir, my necklace." He sticks his hand in the pockets of his black trousers, pulling out the necklace Connor gave me. It dangles from his fingertips as I close the gap, taking the silver strand.

"Thank you," I say, curtly, fastening it again around my neck.

I watch the man as he turns a corner in the trail, seemingly disappearing into the trees.

"Are you missing anything?" I ask Arlan, turning around, my hand still at my throat, playing with the chain.

"No, I don't think so, not outside the coins I had saved and stashed." He sits on the ground and stares at the cooled ashes. "We must've looked like easy targets."

"I agree," I say, pulling a coat out of my bag and shaking the cinders off, brushing them off and leaving long streaks of white. "But, with as short as the days are in this forest, we might as well begin walking." Arlan stands, brushing dirt from his pants. We begin walking, the sound of our footsteps on the cinders spread along the path again the only sound. It fills my ears, but still my hand has not left my necklace. The forest twists and turns and seems to run back on itself. But it doesn't.

"What if we meet the washerwomen again?" I ask Arlan.

"Then we stand our own ground and keep walking, even if it is upon nightfall."

"But what if we meet more thieves?"

"A thief is a thief," Arlan says, nodding at me, "So what if we meet with them or stay with them. All thieves are good for is stealing." I tuck the necklace in my bodice, I feel it bouncing against my heart as I walk. The walk returns to the heavy silence. We eat some of the grain from the bag and pray that we meet a day-town by daylight, all in silence.

To keep travelers safe in this dark forest, there are towns every two days walk, or one day's ride by wagon or horse. In these towns, I've heard that there are places to stay and buy food. We need one of those, or we won't be able to eat, since one of the sinister traits of the Dire Forest is that nothing found within the trees is edible… usually poisonous.

Soon, what little light that can filter through the dense forest cuts off and we are left in darkness. "What should we do?" I ask Arlan, "Now that night has fallen."

"I don't know," he says. He sets his bag down on the ground and lays his head upon it. I am not fond of this idea since the ground is cold and we have no fire.

"There, look," I say, pointing, "Is that the glow of a fire?"

Arlan props himself up with his elbow. “No, Princess, it’s just your imagination.”

“No, I think it is a fire,” I say. The red-orange glow is distinct in the distance, just visible, reflecting off the leaves around the bend. Arlan doesn’t move. He just stares at the thick canopy of leaves woven like fabric above us. “If you aren’t going to go with me, I’ll go myself.” Arlan heaves himself up and grabs his bag, sighing.

The fire comes from around the bend in the trail, but just barely. Arlan and I turn that bend, revealing a group of people, surrounding a glowing fire.

They’re loud and boisterous, playing and shoving, camped on the path. I step off the beaten dirt, into the soft leaves, only half an arm’s length, and go to stash my bag behind it. Just in case this group tries to rob us as well, we won’t chance everything. I try to stand, but my feet slip on the water coating the wet dire-tree leaves. With a swift tumble, I fall behind the log, making a loud sound of leaves on leaves. Arlan’s round, green eyes go wide, and he jumps behind the dark figure of a dire-tree trunk, farther behind me down the trail. We wait, hearts racing, watching the people encamped around the glowing fire. With the sliding sound I made when I fell, they stopped moving, almost all looking up the path, this way. One of the silhouettes stands up, walking toward me. He stops, still on the path, crouching down, gazing through the leaves, through the spaces between them.

"Hey, there," he says, quietly. The group on the path hasn't made a sound since I fell through the brambles. The stranger offers me a hand, and, hesitantly, I take it. It's large and rough, a working man's hand. He helps me up, over the fallen log and onto the path, solid and true. Silently, I walk with him, next to him, toward the group gathered around the fire. Now that I am closer, I see that it's a group of soldiers.

They sit on dire wood logs in a circle around a glowing campfire, nearly identical in light blue wool uniforms with boots and guns by their sides. The brass buttons glow in the firelight. "Hello," says the soldier who pulled me up out of the mud, "I'm Cameron Jones, second division, fifth rank." He brushes his loose, dark blonde curls out of his eyes.

"I'm Georgia," I say, "This is Arlan." Arlan had come out from behind the trees, and now stands next to me, protectively.

"Nice to make your acquaintance," Cameron says, nodding his head in greeting.

"Hey," Arlan says, sitting down on the log next to me. It's soft, rotting with age and wetness, and he puts chinks into it, throwing the chunks into the fire. There they hiss as the moisture is burned off.

"Where are you headed to?" The soldier sitting next to Arlan asks.

"Alyak," he says, staring into the flames of the fire.

"We're on our way toward Jade City. Going home. We just finished our tour," Cameron says. He shifts on the log, and it rolls back a bit until he's settled. "We've got some coffee on the fire, if you want any."

"I'll take some, thank you," I say. He pours some into a tin cup, passing it to me. It's strong, with no sugar or milk to dull the sharp bite. Arlan says nothing. I guess he's quiet this time because the last time he chose our companions, we got robbed. I hope I have better luck than he.

However, I feel much more confident with this group of soldiers than I did with the washerwomen. Partly because our luggage is hidden. And because we can't spend more than one day with them, since we are traveling in opposite directions.

I prepare for a long, silent night, which doesn't happen. One of the soldiers reaches behind the log he's sitting on and pulls out a drum. "I was a Drummer Boy," he says, in explanation, pulling a pair of drum sticks from his pocket. The soldier starts drumming, slow at first, then growing in speed and intensity. It's a tumultuous turn of battle drums and marching cadences, all connected with runs, surely invented in the Drummer Boy's head. The notes are like falling over a cliff, carried only by the falling water.

I stare into my coffee, pray that they don't offer a turn to Arlan. But they do. Arlan takes the drum sticks, adjusting his grip on the worn handles. He begins drumming a tune, I know this one. A series of fast, almost impossibly fast beats, followed by several alternating rim shots and stick clicks and slow beats. I can almost hear the spaces where the tom drummers are supposed to play the tenor toms. The tempo slows to a stop. Then the cadence repeats. It's the tune, dubbed 'The Princess Has Arrived.' My announcement cadence. If these soldiers know anything about the drum court, they'll know who we are immediately.

When the song has stopped, with an elaborate toss of the drumsticks and a final hit, Arlan freezes in the final drum position, before setting the snare down near the fire, and hands the sticks back to the soldier. The group of soldiers are in awe, and silence. "Where did you learn to drum like that?" One of them asks.

"I picked it up somewhere," Arlan says, sitting down and pulling his vinegar-paper notebook, so they'll stop asking questions. But they don't.

"Who are you?" Cameron asks.

“We’re two nobodies from the city,” I say, following Arlan and pulling out my book of poems from my sleeve. Sliding closer to Arlan, I watch the soldiers from the corner of my eyes, and they look at each other, confused. One leans over and whispers something to Cameron, who adjusts his slouch hat and fingers a thin twig pulled from the ground.

The soldier with the drum picks it up again and works on a lick of music, one that he can’t seem to get right. Every time he messes up, he shakes his head, and his long dark hair catches in the wind that tunnels down the pathway. The breeze blows cold on my shoulders, and I let my own hair down to cover them. The dark locks waver in the draft. I pull my coat tighter and sit closer to the fire, though it’s a cold warmth.

Soon, though, the soldiers, who had been talking, start to become quieter as they stare into the mesmerizing flames. I tilt the book toward the dying embers of the fire to catch the last of the dying light, glancing over the top of the binding to catch some of the soldiers nodding off. I look at Arlan, who is adding another log to the fire. He sits down on the log nearest to me, close.

“Do you trust them?” Arlan asks, his voice wafting below the wind.

"At least for now." I stretch my feet toward the fire to chase the cold from the toes of my boots. I rest my head on my arms, closing my eyes and listen to the crackling fire.

****

"Boy," someone says, shaking my shoulder, "Boy. You awake?" I sit up. My neck hurts from being propped up against the log all night, an angle unnatural.

"Hey," Cameron says, his voice low and gruff, "Hey. You and the lass like some breakfast?" I nod, squinting my eyes and rubbing my neck. We're the only ones up. Cameron stokes the fire, hanging the blackened coffeepot above the growing flames. He sets a skillet that he pulls from a bag in the flames, putting a little water in it. When the water beads start dancing and fizzing like the flames in the fire, he lays some strips of meat on the pan. The Princess is still asleep in the space next to me, curled around her skirts, and I shake her. She sighs as she wakes, before sitting up and sitting on the log. Her large purple eyes, examine the fire in the daylight the bacon frying, and the coffee boiling.

The other soldiers, who had been lying, sleeping, haphazardly all over the place, sit up and begin to talk, their gruff voices drifting far above us. Standing and talking, they are walking around and helping themselves to the bacon that Cameron pulls off the skillet and hands out, like a peddler offering wares.

One of the soldiers, I don't know his name, offers me a piece and I take it. It's hot and crispy in my mouth, crunching delightfully. Another soldier, the one missing a few buttons from his blue uniform, offers me a tin mug of coffee, and I take it. I've never had coffee before, and it's a lot more bitter than I expected. Though I don't know what I expected, I've only read about it. We never had coffee in Jasmine Jewel, so I didn't grow up drinking it. Well, neither did the princess, but I've seen her drink it a lot when we go into the city. Some call it pauper's water, because it's so in abundance in the slums and market places.

"Well," Cameron says, "We'd better be on our way. How far is the city from here?"

"Two days journey," I tell him, shaking his hand, "How far until the next day-town?"

"You'd ought to get there about midday," he says, slinging his gun over his shoulder and adjusting the leather strap. The other soldiers do the same afore they roll the logs into the edge of the forest, settling them in the divot on each side of the worn dirt path. The Drummer boy comes up to me, rubbing the wispy stubble on his face and pushing his long hair out of his eyes.

"I won't be needing these in the city," he says, setting the drum by my feet and laying the sticks on top of the head. "I'll just work in my Pa's bakery, and in that bakery, there's no time for drumming."

"Are you sure?" I ask, "Surely, it's got to be worth something."

"It is," the soldier drummer says, slinging his pack over his shoulder and picking his gun up by the strap, "Good day to you."

I nod and wave, as they disappear around the curve and down the path.

"Now, why did he go and do a thing like that?" Princess Georgia asks, spreading out the grey ashes of the fire with the toe of her leather-clad foot.

"What?"

"Leave you that drum. Now we must carry it as well." She raises her eerie purple eyes to mine.

"I'll do it. It'll be no more heavy for you, Princess," I say, "And besides, it has a strap." I lay the drumsticks in my carpet bag, resting the drum on my back and begin the long walk.

Chapter Seven

Cameron was right, we did reach the day-town, even before what we could guess as midday. Our early arrival at the day-town seemed true because not even I could ignore the hunger that was coursing through my body. Everyone thinks that all who live in the castle eat like the king, but that isn't true. It was bread and cheese most days, with some apple cider thrown in during harvesttime. Mayhap some fruit we found between the road and the creek. But, it was still more than Princess Georgia and I have been eating as of late. Which was, to be precise, nothing but coffee, a bite of grain, and a few strips of bacon since the castle.

We walk into the little clearing, bumping up against the edge of the path. A large house features in the middle, with little huts along the outer ring. There are a few pens that rim the clearing that contain pigs and chickens and the like but that's about it. Right in the center of the lopsided clearing is a well, the kind with a draw bucket you lower and raise full of water.

"This must be the day-town," I say to the Princess. She nods, and reads the rough wooden sign nailed above the door of the building. It reads in both Boran and Miran, "Inn." Stepping up to the door, I grasp the brass knocker ring and swing the door open. Inside the dark commons room, there are only two people, the Tender behind the bar and a blind man sitting at a table.

"Good morrow," I say to the Tender, ducking my head.

"Aye, good morrow, lad and lass," he says, stepping behind the desk near the stairs, "Are you here for the night?"

"Yes," Princess Georgia says, "We leave tomorrow."

"Aye, don't they all," says the blind man. He takes another drink of his ale.

I look back to the broad tender behind the wooden counter. "A silver," he says, holding out his hand.

I turn to look at the princess. "I've got it," I say, handing the coin to the man, one last coin that seemed to be overlooked by the thieving washing women. He tucks it in his pocket and hands me a key with a leather tab on it. A Miran number is stamped into it, marking our room number.

"Lad," says the tender, "Do you play?"

I look at the drum, slung over my shoulder. "Yes."

"That piano in the corner," the tender points at a grand wooden thing, falling apart at the seams. "Loren will play that tonight, and if you will drum, and the girl will serve, then your room will be free."

"Why, though?" The Princess asks.

"I have found that happy guests tend to spend more money." The tender shrugs his broad shoulders, and they seem to shake mountains. "Will you do it or not?"

"I'll do it," I say. Begrudgingly, the princess nods her agreement. "What time do we be down?"

"The hour of four," the tender says. "You children look hungry. Take the crusts of the morning meal left unbought." He slides a bundle of food across the worn counter to us, taking it and untying the knot in the material. It's some cold breakfast things, bacon and such.

"Thank you, sir," I say, "But we can't take it." I push the gift across he wooden counter, it seems to slide effortlessly on the polished wood.

“Yes, you can,” the tender says, “I’d have still given it to the pigs, and heaven knows they don’t need it, as fat as they are.”

Princess Georgia takes the bundle tentatively, key still clutched in hand, and gingerly steps up the stairs. It seems as if she places each foot on a predetermined stair spot, perhaps to make sure it doesn’t fall through. I follow her, but take care not to knock the drum on the stairwells or the tight plaster-walled corners, not caring where I place my feet so long as it’s on solid wood.

Our room at the end of the hall is meager, with two cots on opposite corners of the clapboarded floor. Blankets sit, folded neatly, on the foot of them. “I wonder if Tender has a wife,” the princess muses, plucking at the sheet’s neatly folded corners with a nervous hand, “He doesn’t seem the kind to fold sheets.”

“Most likely,” I say, sitting on my bed. I pull out my journal and my quill set and begin to write. My handwriting is awful, and I smear the ink at one point, but at least it’s still legible. Well, more than naught. That’s more than I can say for the writing of last night, by the light of the fire. It was hard to tell what was word and what was shadow.

I look at the drum, set right by my bent knee. It’s a well-made drum, with tight snares on the bottom and a fairly new drum head, barely worn in the middle. The drumsticks in my back pocket poke me, and I pull them out. They're quite unusual; I hadn't really noticed last night by firelight. They're shaped the same, a matching set, and play the same as any others, but it seems that the drummer had painted lightning strikes on them. The blackened line feathers and waves, like the stick had been struck by a bolt. Written along the sides, in neat writing, reads, "Let my strikes be like lightning."

"What are you looking at?" The princess asks, turning her head.

"The inscription on these sticks." I hand her the sticks. She reads the writing along the sides and traces the lightning with her fingers.

Princess Georgia hands them back, and when she doesn't say something and instead pulls out the Bible from her sleeve, I can sense the inelegance in the room. It coats everything like a gauzy sheet of fog, just enough to blur the edges. There was something about spending the night on the trail, with other people, but this is different. It's silent. So much more silent than ever before. I am almost convinced I can hear my own heart beat, although that's not true.

Out of idleness and contempt for silence, I fold the wool blanket into a smaller square and put it on the drum head. This forms a makeshift drum pad, and I practice, every strike making a dull thump, although it was louder than the doeskin. After a while of hearing me practice, Princess Georgia stands up, adjusting her skirts and sweeping across the room. Her skirts trail just behind her as she crosses the clapboard.

She opens the window, swinging the clear pane of glass out. Her heavy boots scrape against the wall as she climbs up onto the wide windowsill and opens her book, one pulled from her sleeve. She is naught but halfway through the book when she says, "Hey, Arlan. Look." I take the drum off my shoulders and walk over to the window. From up here, third story of the house, we can see it getting darker in the paths, but there are no trees above this clearing. It stays light, the sun glowing bright above the grass below. Slowly, we see travelers coming from both directions, walking into the square. Some pay boys to put their animals away, some carry suitcases or bags. A woman in a plain skirt and sash walks through the door, held open by a man in an ornate three-piece suit.

"What's the time?" I ask. Princess Georgia pulls a small watch out of her left sleeve.

"We ought to get going." She swings off the windowsill, her boots thumping across the room. "Are you ready?" I nod and grab my drum. Despite the drum being new, the leather strap is worn, and fits rather perfectly over my shoulder, almost like the strap was worn to me, or my shoulder was carved to fit the strap.

The stairs creak on the long way down, and right as we hit the landing, the tilted grandfather clock in the corner strikes the hour of four. "You barely made it," Tender says, "Loren is already next to the piano."

Sitting at the piano, on the rickety bench, is a man. The blind man, from earlier, the one who sat at the tables. He must be Loren. The pianist turns to me, "Hey, lad, get closer." I step into the corner. "How good are you?" he asks, holding out his hands to pull me closer by the shoulders.

"I've done quite well," I say. I spin the sticks through my fingers, nervously.

"Yes," says Loren, "I know that. But how well?"

"Well enough to be in the Drum Court," I say, "Aged out, though."

"Now did you," Loren leans away, turning back to the piano. That was a lie- I haven't aged out. Won't for another year. And, as I know, Loren thinks so as well. Loren, still facing the sagging piano, says, "Well, then I bet you have done well enough to improvise." I begin to nod, then realize that the old man can't see me.

I open my mouth to say more, but then, a girl about Janson's age steps up to the piano. She sets a roughed-up fiddle on the lid and pulls a chunk of rock to rub her bow. “Good morrow, Loren. How do you fare?”

“Well enough, my dear, well enough,” Loren replies, turning and nodding to her soft voice above the din of the room.

The girl turns to me, “Well, who might you be?”

“I’m Arlan,” I say, “I play the drum.”

“I can tell,” she says, glancing at it. “I’m Rosalind. I play the fiddle.” Loren plays a single note on the piano, and Rosalind props her fiddle to her chin, tuning a somber G to the thick strings. She follows with the other three strings, the other three notes, the other three pegs.

“You ready?” Loren asks, tilting his head. He starts with a lonely note, Rosalind joining in to match it. Then, out of nowhere, they start playing complementing pieces. The music sways, made of fast note runs, a lot faster than I expected it to be.

“You going to play?” Loren asks after a moment, turning his head to my post at the head of the piano. I start, first lying down some basic notes, a flat rhythm beneath the furioso.

****

After Loren and Arlan start playing something fast and lively, Tender comes over. “You ready to start serving?”

I nod. Tender hands me an apron, which I put on. He hands me some mugs of something. "Two bronze a cup. Money in the pocket of the apron." I nod once more, not wanting to say much, lest I be recognized.

As people start drifting in, I start weaving my way through the empty tables. They're pushed together, narrow aisles meant to fit more inside, with the entertainment and ale. A man sits in the far corner. He waves me closer, sliding two bronze across the table, wordlessly. I set a mug down on the wooden top, sliding the coins into the deep canvas pocket of my apron.

As the band begins to play faster, which I didn't think possible, the tables begin to fill up more and more. Soon, it begins to get hard to navigate the aisles, and people sit in chairs. They talk loud, but not loud enough to drown out the music playing from the corner. This style of music, I've never heard it before.

But Arlan does well matching it, does well with the improving capprecio.

A man sits down at a table, beckoning me closer with a wave of the hand. He strokes his beard, tossing me a couple of coins. I set a cup down at the table. "You ever been here before, lass?" he asks. I shake my head.

"No?" He laughs, taking a sip from the mug, "So this is your first time hearing them?" He gestures to the stage.

I nod, warily.

"They're the best music around, the only day-town with a live mountain music band. Though I've never seen that lad before." He takes a drink and begins to talk with the woman that is sitting on the other side of him, something of chickens and winter.

Mountain music, what the man called it. I haven't heard it before, all we hear at the castle are drum cadences and string quartets, playing composers long dead and long buried. I wonder where it came from, and how an old blind man and a young girl came to play it in a small day-town. How long they've been playing, to play so well. I glance toward the stage. The girl is swaying back and forth, sometimes tilting her violin toward the crowd, her long, plain skirts swirling about her ankles as she moves.

I walk toward the bar, picking up one or two more mugs. Tender stops me. "Girl," he says, "We're doing well tonight. People keep asking who the boy is up there. You sure you and your lad don't want to stay here, and work for me?"

"Nigh," I say, shaking my head. "We've places to go." I reach into the pocket of my apron, pulling out a fistful of bronze coins.

“Aye, if you and the lad ever be needing a job, a little one-night thing, come by, you hear?” He laughs, dropping the bronze in tall, crystalline vase behind him. Later, he will probably take the bronze out and hide it, saving it for when sellers come through.

“We will,” I say. I grab the mugs again and head out into the crowd starting to gather at the edges of the small commons room.

Chapter Eight

It was the knock on the door that awoke me. The room was darkened, but sunlight was stretching to get through the cracks of the closed shutters. I sit up on the lumpy cot, drop the woolen blanket on the ground. My skirts settle down about my ankles; I slept in day clothes instead of a night gown. Mother would be horrified. Though, Mother would be horrified with a lot of what I'm doing now.

I move to open the door; Arlan is still fast asleep on his cot. He returned to bed later than I last night, something about settling up with the other musicians. The door swings open with ease and with care. On the other side is the girl who played the fiddle last night. Arlan mentioned that her name was Rosalind, if memory serves well.

"Good morrow," she says, smiling and staring at the lower hem of her skirt. Sitting in the middle of her hand was a single silver coin. "Tender told me to give you this, says you earned your keep last night." I take it from her outstretched palm.

"Good morrow," I say. "Thank you for taking this up."

"It was no problem," Rosalind says. I see her, eyeing my rumpled, sleepy dress. "I'm amazed you haven't got robbed on that trail, dressed as you are."

I look down, first at my dress, then at hers. The dress she wore last night matched mine, with a fuller skirt and bobbed sleeves. Darts had run down the light blue bodice, edged in lace. But now, her dress was a plain grey, tied in at the waist with a simple, matching string. No darts or lace dress up the hems, no buttons or beads to play the neckline.

"We have," I say, "Gotten robbed. They didn't take much."

"Ahh," she says, "We're about the same size, don't you think?" She moves next to me, comparing waist sizes and bust sizes.

"I would believe so," I say. What is she hinting at?

She steps back, slipping her hands into pockets, hidden in the seams of her dress. “Would you engage in a barter?”

“How so?”

“A few of my dresses for yours.” I look once again at her common’s dress and my gown.

That would be quite interesting, and besides, I do need some better clothing. These dresses are much too heavy to be carted around all the time, and I suppose her dresses should be more comfortable than my petticoat-encased entrapments. “I agree,” I say, stepping out of the doorway to let her in.

I open my homemade bag and pull out the few summer dresses I had packed. They spread across the bed, coating it in pastel colors. Beside them, I lay nearly identical underskirts and ruffles in piles.

“You’ve carried these all this time?” she asks, astonished, “Where did you come from? Where you have nothing else to wear but evening gowns?” She looks at me, suspiciously.

“A… very prominent household,” I say, vaguely.

“Must’ve been.” She drapes a pink and a yellow dress over her arm, taking one underskirt and one ruffle to match. “I’d ask you what color of dress you’d prefer, but they are all more or less the same tinge of grey.” She nods, dismissing herself, and walking down the narrow staircase.

"It's barely dawn, and already making deals now, are we?" Arlan sits up on his cot, rubbing the sleep from his eyes before slipping a white shirt on over his bare chest.

"Yes," I say, "How much did you hear?"

"Enough to get the idea," he says, tying his boots on, "And, she was right." I sit down, pulling the two books, handkerchief, and watch from my sleeves. I set them down on the cot. Arlan repacks the few things that he had gotten out, slipping on his suspenders and sticking the drum sticks in his back pocket with his journal. I do wonder what he writes in there.

But, it's then Rosalind returns, rapping a knuckle on the open door. "Here," she says, handing me a few dresses, "a fair trade."

I examine them. "Yes, it is," I say. It's a simple white shift-gown, adorned with a bit of lace at the collar, a matching grey one, and a light blue dress, with a tucked in waist and little other shape to it. However, little shape means less layers, which means more freedom. I turn to Arlan, leaning against the window sill and twisting the drumsticks between his fingers.

"Why don't you go down and buy food for us?" I ask. "I will change here and meet you downstairs." Arlan nods as he ducks out the door, drum strap about his shoulders.

"Well," Rosalind says, "I'd better go and be on my chores or Tender will have my hide."

I nod, closing the door behind her as she steps down the hall.

The grey fabric of the dress Rosalind has given me was smooth against my shoulders, more comfortable than the starched feel of the white gown I was wearing. As I stick my belongings back into my sleeves, I appreciate how the fabric gathers at my elbow and then at my wrist, perfect for storing things. In my old gowns, I used to have to sew pockets in the sleeve belles, lest my books fall out and Mother know what's going on.

This dress feels like something I never got with my castle dresses. It feels like freedom.

Folding the white dress and underskirt carefully, I place them on top of the rest of my clothes in the underskirt bag and pull the drawstring tight around them. I look around the tiny room, to make sure that we didn't miss anything we might need later on.

The common room of the inn was still crowded, part with people leaving, part with people who never actually made it upstairs to their rented room. Tender was busy sticking the leather tags of keys on the nails on the wall behind the bar, returned from customers. I step down the stairs, hand mine to Tender like the rest, and set off to find Arlan.

****

"How much grain until the next day-town?" I ask Rosalind. We are sitting outside, in the crisp morning air, on her wagon. In the back of the wagon were small burlap sacks of grain, which she sells to travelers… like me and the princess.

"One bag of grain, one loaf of bread, one wedge of cheese," she says, "Two silver and a bronze." I hand her the money from my bag, collecting the food-goods from the emptying wagon bed and placing them in my bag, on the top. There's barely enough room for anything else, but I do suppose food should be a priority.

"There you are," Princess Georgia says, stepping through the door to the inn. "Are you ready to go?"

"Yes," I say, settling the thin bag straps over my shoulders. The carpet is heavy with grain, and every time it comes off balance it threatens to tip me over, although heavy food is better than no food, one would rightly argue

"Good morrow, Rosalind," the princess says, starting down the trail to the road, below us in the valley between two hills.

"Good morrow!" Rosalind calls back. I nod to her and follow Princess Georgia down the path. It's tunneled above with the branches of the dire trees, and the path is paved with fallen leaves, forcibly taken down.

The Princess is walking, bag slung over her shoulder, humming quietly. When we've been walking some time, and I begin to feel the bones within each of my ankles rub against each other, I set my drum down. The Princess looks over her shoulder at me, a question in her purple eyes. "Would you like something to eat?" I ask, pulling out the wedge of cheese.

"Yes," Princess Georgia says, nodding and setting her skirt-bag down on the ground. I unwrap the brown paper off of the orange wedge and tear off a chunk from the point.

"For you, my Princess," I say, handing her the cheese.

"Thank you," she says, "But really, you don't need to refer to me like that."

I nod, slowly and focus back on the cheese. I rip off a piece and awkwardly rewrap the wedge, putting it back in my bag, next to the grain and the bread. The silence around us is still uncomfortable, even after three days on the road. I am almost certain it's a sound, or lack of sound rather, that no man can ever get used to. The Princess and I walk down the path, eating our lunch of cheese. Eventually I get lost in my own mind, my own thoughts that swirl like dire leaves towards the ground, and slowly I become more ignorant of my surroundings.

“Woah!” A man’s voice calls abruptly. “Slow down, Amos, or you’ll flip us all!” A wagon comes barreling around the corner we just turned, almost running us over in the middle of the path. It’s naught but a blur. I grab the princess about her waist and we fall, tumbling, into the woods off to the side. We land in the soft leaves that pad the ground behind a fallen log, our legs stuck straight in the air, but the brambles tear at our clothing and hair and skin

“Amos!” The man driving the wagon says sharply, slowing the wagon and jumping to the ground. The man and the wagon have gone past us, but he runs back to offer a hand, taking my wrist and pulling me back on the path, and helping the Princess’s elbow.

“I’m sorry, so sorry,” the man says once we are all upright, brushing his hands on his blue trousers and straightening up, a full height that towers above me. He motions to the horse pulling the wagon. “Ole Amos got going too fast, and almost flipped us twice. I’m Micah Ward.” He glances at his hands before offering them to us in a handshake.,

“Arlan Felix,” I say, taking his hand. He shakes it, if a little overzealously.

“Georgia,” The princess says, shaking his hand as well. I think how the queen would be horrified. Then again, I think how horrified she would be about a lot of things that we’re doing.

Micah turns to his wagon, banging on the side and leaping in the back. I hear voices, Micah’s and someone else’s, too low to understand through the walls of the strange wagon. Then, like a man out of a cave, someone comes out of the wagon that we hadn’t seen before.

He looks like Micah in build and stature, though they have different hair and different faces.

“I’m Nathan Ward, Micah’s my brother,” this new man says, ducking his head towards his feet, “Sorry about almost running you over.” This new man rubs a hand over his jaw.

“It’s fine, sir,” I say, almost ignoring them again as I check the drum for damage before I slide the leather strap back over my shoulder into the divot where it belongs.

“No, really. We feel awful about that. Where are you headed? We could take you there,” the one called Nathan says. Micah steps out of the wagon, climbing over something covered before he jumps down to the beaten path below.

“Alyak,” I say, letting out a long breath. At least these two men look like they’re not going to rob us of our possessions.

"Well, we could go to Alyak," Micah breathes, looking at his wagon.

Georgia steps forward, looking them both in the eyes in a moment of rare-biting rebellion, "No, really. We're fine. You don't need to do that."

"You'd probably get there faster than on foot," Nathan brings up, leaning against the wide side of the wagon and tucking his hands into the pockets of his black trousers. "A few extra days to tour the fine city? Visit Port Calypso?"

I look at Georgia. Her purple eyes are large, and her chin tilts down the slightest bit. I turn back to the brothers, "If you insist."

"Yes," Micah says, his dark curls bobbing gently in the breeze, "it's the least my brother and I can do." With an offering hand, he gestures to the bag in Princess's hands, clutched tight around the drawstring. She holds it out, ever so hesitantly, and he takes it from her, setting it gently in the back of the wagon. He holds out his hand for my bag, and I hand it to him. What else am I going to do? He gently sets it down, behind whatever it is in the back.

"What's that?" I ask, moving to stand closer to Micah, straining to get a glimpse of what lies in the back of this odd wagon. With somewhat of a haphazard grin, he opens the two shutter doors behind the wagon, showing off a box of some sort, only about as wide as it was tall, and spread the length of the wagon's back. With a hand, he reaches underneath it, towards the center, pulling it up and out. Two hidden legs fold down, to help prop it on the ground.

"It's a...," Princess Georgia begins, apprehensive.

"Piano," Micah finishes for her, lifting a long wooden cover to reveal rows of alternating ebony and ivory keys.

Nathan smiles. "We bought the wagon, and Amos too, from a man in a little port by the coast. He said that he had traveled all across the world with this piano wagon, and his band, but then decided to settle down," Nathan says, walking around back and gesturing to the words painted on the side. "He said that he wasn't really Clay Curry, and neither was the man he bought the wagon from. The real Clay Curry made enough to retire years ago and is living in a happy home filled with sunflowers and fiddle music. Or so said the man we bought it from." He laughs.

"Sounds interesting," Georgia says, watching with fascination as the curly haired-Micah lifts the piano back into the back of the wagon, folding the turned legs neatly underneath it. It lifts on metal arms, laden with complicated joints, but goes in without so much as a squeak.

"We'd better get going, if we want to make it to the next day-town by dark." Nathan swings up into the front of the wagon and grabs the reins connecting it to the old horse in front. Micah closes the shutter doors and climbs up onto the roof of the wagon, using hand holds that don't really seem to exist, just one fluid motion from the ground to the roof of the wagon. I follow him up, but using the front bench to pull myself up, and so does the princess. She has no problem swinging up, days of playing ball by candle light has made her strong, though the new skirts trip her a bit, but I doubt anyone but me noticed.

"Go, old Amos," Nathan says, flicking the reins. The wagon starts to creak forward, and for a moment, I'm afraid that it's going to break under our weight.

But it doesn't, and we travel down the twisting path the Dire Forest is famous for. The turns twist back on themselves, and the road seems to spiral into itself as we travel. But, above this muffled, stifling silence, Nathan begins to sing, quietly enough, and Micah lays back on the roof of the wagon. His eyes close and he hums along with the tune that Nathan sings. Soon, the distance between his hums grows closer and closer until they stop. When he begins to slip off to sleep, I lean a little closer to the princess.

"Do you trust them?" I ask.

"Well enough," she replies. "I think they're a faster way to get to Fearless."

I nod. “If you feel comfortable, Georgia,” I say. Calling her just Georgia feels foreign upon my tongue, somehow. I watch the trees go by, watch the trail run underneath us. Sometimes, we’ll pass a place where someone had spent the night, and we’ll know because the trail is stained with the grey-blue of ashes.

But soon enough, I can tell the swaying of the wagon is making Georgia sleepy, like a babe in her mother’s arms. She leans back, grabbing onto the framework molding of the wagon to secure herself, and soon, she is fast asleep as well.

****

“Georgia,” someone says. I crack my eyes open a little, and it takes me a moment to register the covering canopy of leaves above my head. I sit up, blinking the sleep out of the corners of my eyes. It was Arlan who woke me, sitting next to me on the wagon-top. “Georgia,” he says, “The brothers say we’re almost to the day-town.”

I nod.

“Hey, boy,” Nathan says from the bench, “Arlan, aye?”

“Aye,” Arlan says, leaning forward to hear Nathan’s gruff voice a bit better.

"Can you play that drum that you were carrying around?"

"Aye," Arlan says, leaning back once more, his eyes crossed with apprehension.

"Do you want to play with us at the day-town?" Nathan says, just as the day-town comes into view through the opening in the path.

"What do you mean?" Arlan says, pulling his legs in and resting his chin on his knees. "Do you play for money, or for stay?"

"Both, lad," Nathan says, "We play for stay, and whatever else the people will give us pays for food and a rent back home, lad."

It was then Micah decided to sit up out of slumber and join the conversation. "We've played here before," he says, ruffling his own dark curly locks, "They don't have a piano inside. We'll have to play out here."

"Right," Nathan says, looking back. His face is marked with concern, "The Tender might not let us play- playing outside means less money for him, less money for us."

"I could serve outside," I say. I did it in the last day-town, didn't I? "Sell drinks and things like that."

"Lass," Micah says, tilting his head to consider, his brown eyes scanning the dark leaves above, "That just might work in our favor. I'm assuming you don't sing?"

"Aye, no," I say, "I can't sing."

"Lass," Micah says, "Everyone can sing. It's just a matter if it sounds good."

"Well," I say, turning to him, "My voice might just make you change your
philosophy!" They laugh, but it's true. I drove out three singing matrons before Mother decided that I should learn to dance instead. And with those matrons, I didn't even try to drive them out, they just left of their own accord.

"Well, when we use your serving to bargain in with the Tender, we should have no problem getting to play for stay." Nathan brings the Clay Curry wagon to a stop right outside the massive wooden door to the inn.

A boy comes running up. "Misters, shall I put your wagon away for you?"

"That won't be needed," Nathan says, "But we need to talk to the Tender. Might you any idea where he is?"

"Inside, serving drinks, like he always is at this hour," the boy answers dutifully. He turns and heads back whence he came, hiking up his trousers and slamming the barn door behind him.

Nathan steps down from the wagon to the ground below, Micah following him. “It would probably be a good idea if you stayed here,” Micah says to Arlan and I, still atop the wagon, “with the supplies. To keep it safe.”

Arlan nods, scooting back further onto the top. The air feels chilly through the thin grey fabric of my dress, and I cross my arms over me. I didn’t wear a jacket today, it was so warm out. The days are getting warmer, the seasons are changing, but not fully one or another quite yet. It’s stuck in the inbetween… somewhat like us, I suppose.

“Are you cold?” Arlan asks, noticing me pulling my knees to my chest through my skirts.

“Not very much,” I reply. It comes off a little stronger than I expect it too, but oh well. The late remark ends our conversation with a snap, a knife cut, and I search for somewhere, anywhere to focus other than here. Through the amber glass windows of the tattered inn front, we see Micah and Nathan talking to a portly man, probably the tender. After a minute, the door opens to the outside.

“He said he’d let us, if you served,” Nathan says, “We’ll get set up out here, you go inside and see what he wants.”

I slide off the roof of the wagon, climbing down over the driving seat to the hard, dry ground. Inside the Inn, the air is hot with the fire escaping the hearth, set close to the bar. “Are you the girl those singin' men sent?" the Tender says in a gruff voice.

"Aye," I say, wrapping my hands in the apron he hands me, "They told me to meet you."

"Good thing too," he says, "When the people start coming in, I'll tell 'em to go outside."

"What food am I to be selling?"

"You'll sell dough balls and ale. Anything else they want, they need come inside for."

"Aye," I agree, putting the change he hands me into the large, canvas pockets of the apron. Tender seems to be done talking with me, and I am glad to walk out the creaky door to the open air outside. The guys have already set up the wagon off to the side, in between where people enter the clearing and the inn door. They've already pulled the piano out of the back, and Micah sits on the ground beside it, tuning a strange stringed instrument to the lopsided notes spilling from the top. It's not a fiddle, not even shaped the same; this has an odd triangular shaped body and a worn leather strap to go around his thin chest. He's even strumming the strings with his thumbs, instead of using a bow.

After he's satisfied the odd instrument is tuned, he turns to a regular, real fiddle, tuning that to the high plinking sounds of the ivory keys.

"Micah, you done yet?" Nathan asks him, looking back and watching before setting a tip jar up on a stool by the side of the piano.

"Almost there, brother," Micah responds, twisting the last peg a half quarter turn. "There."

I walk over and sit on the edge of one of the grey rocks poking through the soil. There's no one here yet, nothing meaningful to do. I watch the brothers; get a grip on who I will be traveling and working with for the next measure of days.

Nathan runs his fingers over the off-white keys of the keyboard. "Would you climb in back and grab the bench for me? I think tonight's going to be a formal one." Nodding, Micah climbs over the piano, disappearing into the black that is the back of the wagon. A thin black curtain was pulled shut, so people can't see inside, at the brother's personal belongings, one would guess. A moment later, Micah emerges with a small wooden bench, upholstered with black leather, worn through some places. The thin, cracking cover on the bench reveals horsehair, and beneath that, patch-wood.

Still looking at the keys, Nathan reaches up across the piano, and takes it from him. "Thank you, brother," he says, distractedly. And with that, Micah climbs down over the piano, picking up his fiddle and bow from the ground next to the wagon wheel and placing them on his shoulder.

"Are you ready?"

"Whenever you are." Nathan waits a beat before turning to the drummer, saying, "Arlan, we've played together a really long time. Just join in whenever comfortable."

With that, Nathan lays his fingers on the keyboard, and suddenly the air is filled with the fast, rising notes of piano and fiddle. They match one for one, the melody bouncing back and forth. Arlan begins to drum, a slow counter melody to offset the fast pace melody. His beginning beats are clunky and awkward, like he hadn't been on the Drum Court for several years, but with the more measures they put in, the tighter his rolls and the more he begins to sound out.

There's nobody to serve to yet, but still the Clay Curry Band is playing. I remain on my rock, listen to the vaulting music, and think about what we're going to do once we reach Fearless's lair. Since I've the time. It's not like two teenagers could ever take over a world-renowned outlaw- and if the rumors are true, we stand even less of a chance.

I blink, shaking my head, the sound of the tumbling music filling my thoughts once again. People are starting to trickle in, spreading blankets on the ground or just sitting in the back of the wagons they rode in on.

“Do you know who they are, lass?” A woman says from the back of a wagon that just emerged through the tunneled opening of the pathway. “They’re good.”

“Aye, they’re the Clay Curry band,” I reply, taking her money and slipping it in the pocket of my apron. I hand her a string of dough balls, fried and coated with finely ground cinnamon and noraeg, a sweet smelling Miran spice.

“Miss!” someone calls: a young boy, coming closer. “Miss!” He holds out his hands for a sting of doughballs, carefully picking his way around the people sprawled out on the grass. It’s amazing how fast people arrive at these day-towns. When you’re on the trails, you meet people, travelers in passing, but you don’t walk next to them. You feel alone, lost in the twists and turns of the path. They turn to quickly and too often, the trees so dense, you can’t see other travelers. But here, suddenly, you’ve got a crowd of people that appear as though by magic.

I survey all the people that have arrived, in all their different languages and accents, mostly travelers, but some others who live here in the clearing and help with the inn. The people talk and mix, but never loud enough to drown out the band. Women bounce babies on their hips, men talk and tap their fingers on their legs to the beat of the drum. A couple of children, only about eight or nine years of age, sit sideways on a horse, sharing a string of doughballs between them.

Someone calls for another ale, and I'm off to serve them. I pick my way around the blankets and legs of lounging people, spread all into where the aisles should've been.

The song is a fast, mountain sound, ends and leads into a break. The silence isn't uncomfortable, but welcome. The people all around us begin to turn to their neighbors and talk, their voices combining into a hum that offsets everything else. Arlan goes off to get something to drink, and Micah switches to his strange stringed instrument, checking once again it's tuned.

When the short break is over, Nathan stands next to the piano and begins to speak. "Hello, friends. This is not our first time performing at this lovely day-town, but we'll introduce ourselves anyway. I'm Nathan Ward, and this is my brother Micah Ward. Together, we are the Clay Curry band. We play at day-towns all over the country, and are on our way to perform in Alyak. But tonight, we have the privilege of playing with our dear friend, Arlan Felix." Applause breaks, and Nathan clasps his hands, "Donations are welcome, but not necessary. Enjoy the show!" With that, he sits down and plays an amazing baroque lead into a moderate paced waltz.

As soon as the beat settles, couples stand and begin to dance around the outskirts of the crowd. Soon, all the blankets in the middle of the bunch are gathered up and moved away, to make room for the dancers. I see young lads ask their sweethearts to dance, and smile as I hand a pretty woman a string of dough balls.

"Miss, may I have this dance?" says someone, behind me. It's not a low voice but instead a lovely rich tenor.

I turn to see a boy about my age, with his hand outstretched to dance. "Why?" I ask, "I'm just the serving girl." I wipe the brown spice powder on my apron, leaving marring streaks.

"I asked the drummer over there," the boy says, gesturing with his chin, "When they went to break. He told me that you're traveling with them, and that you're serving so they can play. Which makes sense, I've never seen you before."

I pause a moment, tucking a bit of change into my apron. "I would love to dance," I say, taking his outstretched hand and he leads me to the throng of dancers. Rather than a structured dance, as Mother would love to have me learn, this is looser. The same movements over and over again, a simple four- three step waltz. The kind of poor man's dance.

"I'm Georgia," I say. I lay my right hand on his shoulder, and he grasps my left. His hands are calloused, bigger than mine, but gentle.

"Omri," he says. I study his face. He has straight, sandy hair that is just long enough to fall into his kind, blue eyes.

"Omri," I repeat back, "What brings you here?"

"I'm the stablemaster's son," he says as we dance, "I was raised here, and I've never seen anything else. But one day, one day I'll travel- and see distant cities and maybe even other countries." His eyes sparkle with the wish and the firelight.

"I've only joined the Clay Curry band since Jade City. But, I've always heard that Jasmine Jewel is a lovely place," I say, and the music pauses, a caesura, the spot for a turn and a dip.

Omri opens his mouth to say something, but with only a few short steps, the song ends there with a cascade of fluttering notes down the scale. "Thank you for that dance," I say, dipping into a slight curtsy, as is the custom.

He nods, before bowing, his blue eyes twinkling in the orange light coming from the day-town lanterns. "It's my pleasure. Maybe, if you pass through again, I could see you?"

"That would be lovely," I say, "but, I really must get back to work." I pick up my apron off the rock that I laid it on, and untangle the strings.

"No, let me," he says, taking them and tying them behind my back, out of the way. I smile as someone else calls for ale, and he nods his head, his shaggy blonde hair, and heads towards the stables.

The rest of the night, I keep thinking about the dance, and Omri. What will become of him? Will he ever leave, or will he stay and pick up his father's job of Stablemaster? Does Omri want something more?

Does it matter?

Chapter Nine

****

We play late into the night. Late enough that all the women pack their children up to go to bed, stashing them away inside the inn, and all the men too full of ale have fallen asleep where they sat outside. The stars shine bright above, like beacons into the inky blue night. And after the music has stopped from the last song played to a sleeping audience, the tender comes out and tells us that it was two in the morning, and that we could go to bed, if we wish. That we had certainly made enough money for him to earn a room inside.

"Thank you," Nathan says, shaking the large, round bellied inn Tender's hand. This Tender had seemed rugged and brutal before, but now he was sleepy. The veil of sleep made him seem like a gentle giant.

"Anytime," Tender says, "Here's the key to your room." He hands a leather tabbed key, similar to the one that the princess and I got at the last day-town, to Micah before yawning broadly and going back inside the dark building.

"Georgia," I say to the princess. She had sat down on the piano bench and fallen asleep with her head across her arm, crossed over the keys.

Almost hesitantly, she raises her head, blinking her large purple eyes, looking around at the quiet night around us. "What time is it?" she asks, blinking her eyes once more and pushing the hair away from her face.

"The clock just struck two. You'd best off to bed; I'll help around here." I hold out the key to her, the brazen metal dangling from the leather fob. She looks at it, like her mind isn't processing what's going on right now. It probably isn't, anyway.

"Take it," I say, lowering it into her opened palm. She blinks once, twice, before crossing the clearing, the white lace darts incandescent in the star shine.

"She's not used to late nights, I take it," Micah laughs, "Naught was I at the beginning."

"Nor I," agrees Nathan, putting the horsehair bench into the back of the wagon.

"Have you just learned to live with less sleep?" I ask, trying to stifle a yawn that raises from the depths. Nathan and Micah seemed as awake as they were when we had first met them.

"No, my lad," Micah says, lifting the piano into the wagon, "We sleep during the day. Whilst we're on the road."

Nathan moves to close the shutter-doors of the wagon, before he realizes I still have my drum. "Do you want to store it in the wagon as well?"

I hesitate. Would they steal it? Would someone else? It hasn't left my side since I got it, the strap has carved a place into my shoulder and I can't lose it.

"It'll be safe, I promise," Micah assures, seeming to sense my qualms. Waiting only a moment more, I hand it to him, and he sets it behind the piano. The shutter-doors, pale in the moon, close over that, locked in place with a large padlock. I see Nathan stashing the silver shining key in his pocket.

"We'd best be getting to our rooms," Nathan says, "We've an early morning."

"An early morning!" I say, incredulously. "It is morning."

"Fair enough," Micah says, opening the door, "Good morrow, then."

The only people left in the inn lobby are those who work here and those passed out, slumped over half empty tins of staling ale. We turn down a hallway, passing closed oaken doors. Unlike the last inn, the layout of this one is spread out, sprawling even. After several turns and right passages, we reach our door, and Nathan slides the spare key in the lock. It sticks a little, requiring much effort to turn, but we get the door open, displaying the dark, yawning room.

There are only two cots, and one is taken by Georgia. She fell asleep on top of the covers, her stockinged feet splaying off the end like a doll's.

"Now what?" Micah asks his brother quietly, "There aren't enough cots."

"I know," he says, rubbing his chin thoughtfully. "I'll go back out to the wagon and use the sleep-away."

"I'll take the sleep-away," Micah says, moving towards the door, "I'm younger."

"I'm older. You sleep on the floor in here, make a mattress out of blankets." Nathan says, "Just don't forget to open the window." To prove a point, he grabs the spare key and turns out the door, disappearing before anyone else could object.

With his head inclined, Micah moves across the floorboards to the window, opening the shutters wide. The night outside is inky with darkness, naught but bats and bugs flying by in the silken moonshine. "To wake us in the morning."

I nod. We used to do the same thing sometimes, in the drum court… if we had someplace to be in the morning and no use of alarms. We oft slept through it even so.

Micah picks up the blanket off the remaining cot, to make his bed, folding it over to thicken it.

"No, I'll take the floor," I say to Micah, before he could spread it on the splintery boards, "I'm smaller, I could use less blankets."

"No really, I insist, we almost ran you over…" Micah breaks off.

"I know, and you've repaid in full. More than full. Taking us here was enough for that. I'll take the floor," I argue. Georgia stirs in her bed, pulling her arms closer about her chest, eyelids fluttering. Micah and I stop moving, making sure we don't wake her. She sighs once more, before relaxing her arms and her eyelids.

I look at Micah, standing by the window, poised to spread the blanket.

"I'll take the floor," I say quietly, but solid enough to make Micah agree with me.

"Here's the blanket," he says, handing me the one he was holding. "I'll just use the sheet." The blankets worn wool, but it's thicker. I take the spare from the rack above the second cot, lay it on top of the other. It's thin, and uncomfortable, but no more than the cot I slept in in the last town.

I pull my jacket off to make a pillow, and lay that on the top of the blanket bed. My shoulders are bare, covered in goose bumps, but I care not to use one of the blankets below me to cover them. I lay quietly on top of the makeshift mattress. Gravity pulls on my bones, relaxing my muscles as sleep tears at the corners of my eyes.

But the sweet sleep doesn't last. Soon, the window is full of sunlight and Micah is up and moving about the room, making noise. The sun is barely up in the sky, too early to be up after such a late night.

"What time is it?" Georgia yawns, sitting up and wiping her eyes.

"Half past the hour of six, my lass," Micah says quietly, slipping on his boots. The distressed leather soles are worn almost through in the heels, the sidesoles bent sideways over the edges, a sign he doesn't walk quite right.

With what little thought process I can cobble together, I notice I must've slept in all my clothes, so I lace my boots back on. Georgia props her chin in her hands on her elbows, blinking her big purple eyes several times.

There's a knock on the door, but then the lock clicks and the door swings open. Nathan steps into the room. "Good morrow," he says, smiling and setting the shadow of a hunk of salted ham onto the table.

"Good morrow," Georgia replies, looping the laces of her boots around her ankles to shorten them, brushing her dark curls away from her eyes before standing up and rearranging her skirts.

Nathan breaks off a piece of ham, handing it to me. It's salty and dry, nearly inedible, but it's what we've got. He hands a chunk to the princess… Georgia.

"Thank you," Georgia says, taking a bite out of the red meat.

Micah looks around the crumpled room. "Well," he says, "We're ready to go?"

"Aye, brother," Nathan says, reaching for the door. He opens it, stepping out into the long, dank hallway. It's empty and quiet, save the occasional snore from an occupied room.

We make our way into the main lobby, empty as well. There's light coming through the windows positioned in the corners, catching every bit of dust floating amongst the empty chairs at empty tables.

"The Tender's not up yet," Micah says, looking at his brother with a sidelong glance, "Shall we wait?"

"I don't know," Nathan says, "We need to get going." Almost as if he's afraid to make too much noise, he sets the leather tabbed key on the bar counter before moving toward the door, resting his hand on the washed bronze of the handle.

Just then, the Tender comes from the back, appearing from the dimness of the back room. "Are you leaving already? Not even staying till morning meals are ready to be served?" He hangs his hand on his neck, pulling a strip of flour cloth from his shoulder and wiping the counter.

"Aye, sir," Nathan says, "We have best be going, if we're to make it to the next day-town before nightfall." He hands the key to the Tender. Tender hangs the key on the rack behind the counter, right in its labeled spot.

"Well," Tender says, "If you're ever in town again… stop by. Play a bit. That girl you got there makes a haul with her serving." He nods towards her.

Nathan and Micah look towards Georgia. She smiles inelegantly and looks down, leaning toward me the tiniest bit, as if the weak strains of gravity were pulling on her. "Well, then, we'd better be going," Nathan says. He and Micah shake the Tender's hand, but before I get a chance to, the tender turns around. He stretches and scratches and steps back behind the counter and into the kitchen.

"Well, that was pleasant, wasn't it?" Micah grumbles as he hitches Amos to the wagon. I don't blame him- some tenders are better than others, but this one did seem rough. But, being a tender is a hard job, not many take it. Most are born into it and unable to escape.

I notice that the lock is undisturbed on the wagon, which pleases me. I'm glad that the drum wasn't stolen; it's the way we've been traveling the last few nights. But, the air is still damp from the morning dew, and the sun is barely above the tops of the dire trees.

"You'll drive, won't you?" Nathan says to Micah, sounding tired and handing him the reigns to old Amos. Micah nods solemnly, and Nathan swiftly unlocks the back doors to the wagon. He climbs inside the yawning belly of it, and I feel the wagon shift with the weight of him settling beneath Georgia and I.

Micah leans foreward, elbows on his knees, slowing the wagon down. "Go, go to sleep," he says, "I'll make sure we won't go too fast. You won't fall off." He guides us through the edge of the clearing and onto the dusty path.

But, as soon as we start going down the trail, I lay my head down on my arms. I stretch out longways atop the wagon, my arms crossed in front of me, my eyes staring at the road. Amos is walking like he doesn't need anyone to tell him where to go, like the reigns don't do much good after all. The clouds above me trade out for the limbs of trees, and the rays of sunlight slowly disappear. Once we reach the first turn into the forest and you can't see the day-town anymore, I shift. Close to the front of the wagon is my head, propped on my arms, but my feet hang off the wagon top at the ankles. My feet move with the swaying of the wagon, turning and jostling.

With my eyes closed, I just listen. The woods are silent, only the sound of Amos's hooves on the dirt and ashen pathway. I hear fabric rustling, and I know that Georgia is settling down to sleep beside me. Soon, I hear her breaths, deep and steady, as she falls asleep.

After a while, Micah starts to sing. The words get left behind the moving wagon with no one to hear them but I. And soon, not even that, for I fall asleep to his baritone tune.

****

After we're all awake, and the wagon has picked up speed once more, Nathan pulls food from his oil-leather pack. There under the trees, we eat a meager meal of bread and cheese, the food of paupers. Cheese pried from a wedge wrapped in vinegar paper, to preserve it, and bread, staled with two day's journey in a paper bag. We eat on the moving wagon, swaying as we travel too fast around curves, keeping our food close lest we lose it to the speed of the barreling wagon. But, just as we finish out meal, and Nathan packs the food away, that's when it starts to rain. Rain in the Dire Forest is a peculiar thing- it doesn't fall from skies but from the leaves. With these raindrops comes wet greenery and moss from the branches above, making the whole experience thoroughly miserable.

A clump of moss lands on me, on my lap. It's raining vegetation. Micah, still driving, pulls a little rain shield that's folded into the front of the wagon. The fabric, treated with waterproof oil, lets the rain and moss slide right off it. The three of us, however, aren't as lucky.

"Usually, when it rains, I would go and climb into the wagon," Nathan says, resting his arms on his knees and wiping a bead of water from his eyes. "However, the three of us won't fit in there with all the musical supplies." He seems apologetic, at least somewhat, as he shakes water from his curly mane.

But, as any commoner would tell you, rain in the Dire Forest also means slow going. Animals can no longer go any faster than a careful walk, lest they slip and break a leg. Even if you did manage to pick up speed, the wheels would get stuck in the clay -rich sludge and break. Then, you would be stuck out here for longer. So, we just had to sit there and wipe half rotten, soaking wet leaves from our brows and wait for the next turn, for the next puddle, the next almost-river to ford through in our piano-wagon.

As anyone would think, it was a relief when we turned that last turn on the road and found ourselves looking at a day-town.

It was a tragedy, though, when we realized the inn had no roof

"What will we do?" I say, "There's no place to stay." The inn was wet through and through, nothing inside but new walls and no roof. No guests, no tender, no people. It was seemingly abandoned. I feel the tears pulling at the corners of my eyes, tearing at the edges.

"Aye," Nathan says, rubbing his face, his eyes. "We need a place to stay, dry and warm."

"Well," Arlan said, choosing his words carefully, "We could... sleep somewhere we weren't invited." His eyes glance around the clearing, through the rain now falling from the sky.

"What do you mean by that?" Micah says, sullenly shaking the water from his damp curls.

"Look," Arlan says, his voice low, "We could break in somewhere and sleep. Not steal anything, but just...you know, stay dry."

The brothers are silent, same as I. We just stare at him and stare at each other.

Finally, Nathan speaks, to break the silence. "If we're going to break in somewhere, let's not make it a house."

"No," Micah agrees. He looks thoughtful, "How about a church?"

"A church?"

"Aye," Micah says, "No one will be there, it's naught but Saturday. So long as we're gone by morn tomorrow, there'll be no trouble."

"If it's the best plan we've got," I say. I'd stay anywhere right now, just to be able to change out of these skirts. They're soaked through with water and threatening to pull down at any second.

"How are we going in?" Nathan asks, "We right as well all can't go waltzing through the front door."

"This is true," Arlan says, rolling up his sleeves, "One of us can go through the front door, let the others in through the side."

"Who shall it be, then?" I say.

"It'll be you," Arlan says, looking at me. "No one will suspect a lass, going into church to pray. Not with a scarf about her head, not with her wet skirts wrapped tight."

"Aye," Nathan agrees after a moment. He offers his hand to help me climb down off the top of the wagon, and I take it. My feet slip out from underneath me, sliding on the wet wood of the wagon, but I catch myself soon enough, landing square on the ground. There's no one around as I walk to the middle of the clearing. I watch as Micah leads and ties Amos and the wagon to a tree in a deserted corner of the clearing, and they hurry over, crushing under the eaves of the white walled church.

"Go," Arlan mouths to me. I step through the front doors of the church, heavy oak ones decorated with carvings of grapes on branches and serene looking lambs. On the inside of the small, white church everything is dry and warm and quaint. At one end of the meeting room lies an organ, its pipes reaching high into the ceiling. On either side of the organ are large, purple stained-glass windows, lining the walls and casting a serene glow over the rows of pews between me and the stage. Off to the side is a stove, meant to heat the room. With as warm as the air is in here, I'd bet the priest just went home, expecting no visitors this evening.

To the side of the stove is a door, going to the outside. I open it, and the heavy wood moves swiftly on its well-oiled brass hinges. The guys are leaning against the side wall of the church, trying to stay under the overhang of the church's roof. "What took you so long?" Micah says, teasing. I smile back, twisting it to mimic his elfish grin. My skirts squish against the paneled wall as I move aside, to let the guys into the warm room. When Nathan and Arlan are in and Micah's the last out, I start closing the door.

"Let you stay out longer for your impudence!" I say, in a mock scolding tone, a smile across my face. Micah laughs, and I let him in. He shakes his head, throwing water onto me.

Nathan is gazing at the giant pipe organ. "It's huge, the biggest I've ever seen," he says. He moves his fingers, and I can tell he's just itching to play it. I mean, I am too, and I don't even know how to play.

Arlan has already curled up by the stove. He lies his dripping clothing on it, hoping to dry them quicker.

"You'll take the warmth from it if you keep it wet," Micah says, looking at him.

“I know,” Arlan says, his eyes downcast, searching for something. From the box on the side, he pulls a log of dire wood, only about as thick as his bony wrists. Slipping a knife from his pocket, he swiftly strips the bark from the circular log. They fall in long curls, ribbons of the thin, papery bark. Opening the door to the wrought-iron furnace, he sets the log into the pink coals. When he realizes that we’re staring at him, eyes open wide, he says, “It’s the bark in the dire wood that makes it smoke so much. The heartwood doesn’t smoke much at all.”

“Now, where’d you learn that?” Nathan asks, resuming the chore of peeling off his socks and his shirt.

“Nowhere,” Arlan says, moving to sit on a pew in the front row, “Books, I guess.”

“You learn a lot from them?” Micah asks, pulling off his shirt as well.

“I guess I do.”

The room is silent, save Nathan already stripping more bark from the dire wood. I am glad I chose to wear a skirt and blouse instead of a dress now, because I take off the thick petticoat and the overskirt and just walk around the warm church in my linens. In the summer, I resent the full skirts you’re supposed to wear in courts, because they trip me up when I’m trying to run, and get in the way when I try to swim in the creek. Hooks get caught in the fancy laced bottoms when we fish, and Mother gets mad when I rip one climbing a tree or the lattice. But, during the winter, skirts are a lot warmer than trousers. More layers available.

"So, Nathan," I say, sitting on the stairs with my dark hair to the now blazing open furnace door, "If we're to be stuck here, we might as well get to know each other. Have you got any family? Any wife or daughter?"

"Not me," he says quietly, serenely. "I never was one to settle down. Now, Micah, he's another story."

"Micah," I ask, turning to him, "Have you got a family?" Micah is thumbing through one of the hymnbooks he found on the back of a choir chair.

"What's that?" he asks, looking up, "Have I got a family? Well, yes, indeed I do. But that's a long story."

"We've got the time," I say.

Nathan sighs. "Don't push it. Micah, you don't have to tell them."

Micah sets the hymnbook back down, sitting next to me on the stairs to the stage and the stove. "No, it's fine."

"Really?"

"Yeah. Ready for the story?"

We're all quiet, waiting for the story. "There was a girl, I fell in love with her. Head over heels, never stopping love.

Back when we were young," he starts, and we settle down into his story. "Her name was Alayna. Alayna lived with her father in the little town close to me, down by Port Seaware. You know where that is? Down by the sea, of course. Well, when we were a little older, her father and she moved to the city, so he could get work. It was about a year after that; a drunk little man came to town and offered to sell us the wagon. We bought it, Nathan and I, and we began playing in city squares in Jade City. While we were there, cleaning up after a show in a marketplace, a man came up to us." Micah pauses, pulling his knees in closer. "He said he was Alayna's father, and that he married her off because he couldn't pay to feed her, and that the man wasn't very kind to her. He said that she needed someone to take her away from there, take her somewhere safe."

Here, Nathan interjects. "He also said that she had a child," he says gruffly, sticking another piece of wood on the fire.

"Aye, that too," Micah says, his arms waving as he animates the story in the air above us. "He left and came back a few minutes later, leading my Alayna by the hand. In her arms was a little girl, hiding her face. We put them in the back of the wagon, hidden, and took them to a day-town, riding through the night."

At this, I see Arlan look up from his journal in which he was furiously writing in moments before, entrapped in Micah's morose story.

"We brought them inside, paying for a room. Her father had given us some money, enough to pay for a few nights there. I..." here, his voice cracks. "I had to leave Alayna and her daughter there." Micah explains, "It's safer for her there, than with me and Nathan, traveling through the forest. But, I stay for a few days when we pass through, and bring money back for her and her daughter. They both work there at the inn, though, so they don't really need it." He laughs sadly, his voice drooping. "I'll marry her one day, though, I swear."

"Aye, you mean what you say?" Arlan says. He hardly talks, so when he does, we all stop to listen.

"Of course, lad, why would I tell you wrongly?" Micah asks.

"It's just that we played there, with her. She plays the fiddle, yeah? Accompanied by a blind pianist, Loren?"

"Aye," Nathan says incredulously, "Have you met her?"

"Met her? I played with her," Arlan says.

"Tell you the truth?" Micah asks in disbelief, turning to Arlan, leaning toward him, "Did you see Alayna?" His face is like a small child's.

Arlan shakes his head, turning back to his book, almost apologetically.

"Micah," I say, "Did you teach her to play?"

He turns back to me, resting his spidery hands on his knees. "Aye," Micah says, laughing a little, "Is she really that good?"

"I would say that she is." I pull the ribbon from my hair, letting the wet strands trail down my back to length, letting the stove heat bake them dry.

"Here," Nathan says, pulling some food from his bag. He tosses the bread to Micah, hands some hard cheese to me. I break off a piece from the tip, handing the wedge to Arlan, who had already put down his book and was sitting by the stove with the rest of us.

"So, Arlan," Nathan says, joining us on the floor. He sits, completing the circle, and Nathan hands him the loaf of bread. "Where did you learn to drum like that?"

Arlan pauses, looking at the drum in the corner, "My brother was a drummer, and he taught me."

"A drummer," Micah says, "where did he learn? Was he a drummer boy in the army?"

"Aye," Arlan says, "he taught me everything he knows." He says this and turns back to his book. I know it's so they won't keep asking questions.

"You must excuse him," I say, "He's not one for talking much."

"I can see," Nathan says, throwing another log on the fire. By now, the large church room is warm and we're all comfortable and sleepy, stuck in the inky blue darkness of the small and quiet church.

That is, until we all hear the door slam.

"Dear God in heaven," Micah whispers as a somewhat rumpled man bursts into the room.

****

"Oh, Lord," the Priest says, pausing in the doorway. "I thought that I had left the fire going. Never in my sixty-seven years did I think that someone broke in."

"I'm sorry, sir," Nathan says, standing up. He grabs Georgia's wrist, pulling her to her feet and filling her arms with partly dry clothing from the stove. "We'll be going. We didn't think anyone was here…" he trails off, picking up his kerchief bag and going to the door.

"No, no, my lad, it's quite alright. You don't seem to be full of malice in nature," the Priest says, "And I'm sure you just came in because of the rain, and that the inn is… out of business." The priest begins to walk down the aisle of pews, taking some clothes from Georgia and spreading them back out on the stove.

“Really though,” Nathan says, taking the clothes off the stove again. “We must be going.”

“No, I insist,” the priest says, “You must stay here. You’re not disturbing anyone, and just until morning.” His voice rings out against the silence of the room, the sound bouncing off the back wall and to us.

“Are you sure, sir?” Micah asks.

“Of course I’m sure,” the priest says, “Look, it’s already dark out. You can’t travel at night in these forests, surely you know that.” Nathan nods in hesitant agreement, setting his kerchief bag back on the fire box. “Just the night,” the priest insists again.

I hadn’t moved much, maybe just scooted back a mite amongst all the commotion. Georgia comes and sits next to me once again, tucking her bare feet under her and piling her hair up on the top of her head in a loose pile. She stabs the roll of it with a twig from the fire box to hold it in place, up off her neck. Strings of still damp hair trails down from the roll, like a ball of yarn.

Hesitantly, Nathan sits next to the stove, resuming the place where he was before. Micah sits on the other side, restoring our tentative circle.

"Who are all of you?" The priest asks, sitting in the front row of the church. He rests his hands on his knees, leaning forward.

"Oh, we're naught but performers," Nathan says, quickly, wringing his hands and looking down.

The priest laughs. "You, my friend, I like you. I meant, what are all your names?"

"I'm Micah Ward, this is my brother Nathan," Micah says. Then he looks at us, not really sure how to introduce us, nor how to explain how we know each other.

"I'm Arlan," I say. Georgia is already folded in upon herself, seemingly, trying to hide her face. "This is my sister, Alayna."

"Arlan and Alayna," the Priest says, hearing them together, "I'm glad to have met you. I'm Brother Gaius Mahoney."

"Well, Brother Mahoney," Nathan says, eyeing us, "Surely, we could repay you for your hospitality."

"My son, my son," Brother Mahoney says, "Not everything comes with a price."

"But…" Nathan says, but he can barely get a word in before Brother Mahoney interrupts him.

“I simply try to do the work of God,” he says, “But if you really feel so indebted to me, you could stay for service tomorrow.”

“Of course, if you’re sure there’s no more we could do,” Nathan says.

“I’m quite sure,” Brother Mahoney says, “Not unless one of you could play the organ.” He says this disbelievingly, like he wasn’t prepared for us to be a band of traveling musicians.

“Are you telling the truth?” Micah asks, “You need someone to play the organ?”

“Well, yes,” Brother Mahoney says, looking confused, “That one’s not been played for years, not since the last organist died of influenza, poor soul.”

“Brother,” Micah says, standing, his arms spread wide, “We’re a band of musicians, traveling musicians that play from town to town. I play the fiddle, Nathan plays the piano, Arlan here drums and… Alayna… serves the tables for us. We usually play in exchange for rooms at day-town inns.”

“In that case, there is something you can do for me,” Brother Mahoney says, “Nathan, to ease your troubles, I would be honored if you were to play the organ for the congregation tomorrow.”

"I would be honored to play," Nathan says, crossing the room and shaking the old man's hand.

"Well," Brother Mahoney says warmly, "I'd better be going home. These old bones don't do well with being up late, especially in cold and rain such as this. Have a pleasant evening." Brother Mahoney stands, seemingly with much effort, and walks back down the center aisle and out the front door.

We hear the heavy doors click with a loud latching sound.

Then there's a beat of silence. I feel the cold air from outside wash around me and wait to hear what happens next in this dark room.

I hear a deep breath. "I want to know what's going on," Nathan says firmly.

"I don't know what you're talking about," Georgia says, pulling her book of poems from her sleeve and holding them in front of her face.

"You and Arlan aren't siblings and your name is certainly not Alayna," Micah says, reaching out and gently pushing the book down from Georgia's face. "What the heck is going on?"

"Well," Georgia says, "If we tell you, you must keep this a secret and still take us to Alyak, despite what you think is right."

“I can’t agree to that,” Nathan says, eyebrows knit together in frustration. He studies us, his eyes darting from face to face.

Another beat of silence.

“I can,” Micah says, “What are you saying? Tell us the truth.”

I look up from studying my hands. “Did you ever hear about the Drummer that was kidnapped by Fearless Le Paige?”

They nod. “It was all over the papers a while back, what… three months ago? Something like that?” Micah says, leaning forward.

I nod. “Well, I’m another drummer and I’m setting out to rescue him,” I tell Micah and Nathan. There’s enough time delay that they would’ve heard about Janson’s disappearance, but not about Georgia’s and mine, especially with them traveling.

“He’s another drummer, then what are you?” Micah says, turning to look at Georgia, “A scullery maid?”

“I’m the king’s daughter,” Georgia says, “Princess Georgia of Bora.” She says this somewhat defiantly, enjoying the mixed looks of horror and surprise on Micah’s and Nathan’s darkened faces.

“Well, then,” Micah says, once the shock has somewhat worn off his face, highlighted in the light of the fire, “Just my luck. Who else could've I run over than the Princess?" He buries his thin face in his hands, pulling at his hair, rubbing his cheeks in frustration.

"Oh, Lord," Nathan says, "You mean you've been serving drunk old men for money to stay in broken down day-towns with two complete strangers, and you're the *princess*."

Georgia nods.

"You mean you're sitting here in, in a church we broke into, in mud stained, dripping wet linens and you're the *princess*."

"Yes," Georgia says. "I also rode through the rain on the back of a wooden wagon with a piano in it, pulled by an ill-tempered horse named Amos, and I'm the princess." I smile a bit at her mocking them. But the smile's short lived, it's but the next crucial lines that will decide where we go from here. I pull my knees tighter around me and look around the dark room.

"Well," Micah says, "I guess we're too far to turn back now, aye." His voice catches again, his brown eyes shining in the orange fire light, like beams in the darkness.

Nathan is too dumbfounded to speak. Finally, he clears his throat. "I guess that's where you learned to drum so well," he says, but the look of shock still rings clear across his face, cast with frightening shadows from the fire in the stove.

And it is there that we sit, in the silence, staring at the slowly dying fire and listening to each other breathe. Nobody says anything, but Georgia stands up and pulls a cushion off the front pew, untying the knots that hold it there and lying it down next to the stove. I stand and pull the cushion off another, and so does Micah. The cushions are of a rough blue fabric, the strands shot through with other colors, as if it was of a home-made hand. As it probably was. But Nathan doesn't fetch his own pew cover, he is already asleep, or at least he pretends to be, spread out on the thinly carpeted stage, next to the pulpit.

Tonight, sleep doesn't come quick. It's a lazy and impatient thing, sleep, something that comes too quickly some nights, and not soon enough others. Although, maybe I'm dreaming that I'm not sleeping; one never knows how his dreams will turn out. I close my eyes to the darkened church and listen to Georgia's breathing and the crackle of the fire. I listen to them slide in and out of synchronization.

And sometime between then and morning, I fall asleep.

Chapter Ten

"Arlan," Georgia says, kneeling next to me, "Arlan, are you awake?"

I nod, blinking the sleep out of my eyes and waiting for them to adjust to the bright light streaming through the purple windows. Micah is still asleep, sprawled out on his cushion. Either that or he's awake and procrastinating, but Nathan is already up. He's standing by the stove, putting on suspenders and combing his hair by the somewhat distorted reflection in the purple windows.

"He says he should be presentable when he plays the organ," Georgia whispers, leaning closer towards me. She's already dressed in something different- back to her white dress this time. Gone is the twig that held up a knotted braid of hair. Now her dark curls are tied up with a short length of twine, although she looks like a traveler who decided to get dressed up to come to church. The lace lining the bottom is traced with mud, which helps the picture as well. "You'd best get dressed," Georgia says, standing up and putting a cushion back on a pew it probably didn't come from.

Next to my cushion, there lies my carpet bag. My pants are mostly clean- they ought to be, after all that time in the rain- so I just change my shirt. I put on a new white shirt and a black vest that I didn't know I packed with me. Almost absentmindedly, I run my fingers through my hair only to find that the water has stuck it together and that it has dried at exceptionally odd angles. Such is life, I think, licking my palms to try to smooth it anyway, in a somewhat futile attempt.

The door opens at the end of the hall with a loud crashing sound like the one last night. Those doors must need new hinges or something. His arms laden with bread, Brother Mahoney makes his way down the aisle. "Good morrow," he says, handing a loaf to me, "I suspect you could use something to eat on this lovely morn."

"We're fine, really," Nathan says, "We've brought food of our own."

"No, no, no," Brother Mahoney says, "I insist. Look, I even have fresh butter and honey- if you don't eat the bread and butter, it'll go bad and then no one can use it." To prove a point, he aptly butters a slice of bread, dribbles a bit of honey on it and hands it to Georgia.

"If you insist," she says, ducking her head. A bit of honey rolls off the slice and onto her chin as she eats it.

"Delightful, isn't it?" Brother Mahoney asked, "It was freshly harvested and brought in as tithe by one of my parishioners. Why don't you all put your stuff away- didn't you say you had a wagon somewhere? – and get ready for service. It starts in a little while."

"What do you want me to play on the organ?" Nathan asks, picking up the hymnbook from the chair.

Brother Mahoney stands next to Nathan at the piano, flipping pages through the hymnbook. "Here," he says, putting the book on the music stand on the organ, so Nathan can see it.

"This one?" Nathan asks, pointing to a spot on the page filled with lined staff.

"Aye," Brother Mahoney says, "That's my favorite. Don't butcher it, please." Nathan laughs and starts playing a church tune, just a tad too slow. His foot stumbles over the many petals lining the floor, and the music comes to a stop.

“You must forgive me,” Nathan says, “It’s been a while since I’ve played an organ. Mostly, it’s just piano.”

“No,” says Brother Mahoney, “Don’t be sorry. This congregation hasn’t heard an organ in so long, they’ve probably forgotten how one sounds.” He laughs and turns the page, pointing out a couple songs that should be played for today.

Nathan starts playing again, but soon the sound fades out. “It wasn’t me this time, Brother,” he says, staring at the keys like they’ve failed him.

Brother Mahoney laughs again. I think how odd it is to find someone this jovial in such a dreary day-town. “It’s no one’s fault,” he says, “except maybe the organ boy. He’s the one in charge of keeping the bellows full. But no one can blame him- he married near twenty years ago and moved oft to the city.”

“I’ll pump the bellows,” I say, standing on the treadle by the edge of the organ. I swap my weight from one foot to the other, and air starts to screech through the pipes. Brother Mahoney flips a knob in front of me, and the sound condenses until it forms a single note- one that matches the key that Nathan is holding down.

“There,” Brother Mahoney says, “now you can play.”

And he does. Music notes flow out of the keyboard and into the air. The pipes vibrate and the ones with the lowest notes almost seem to want to break free of the ceiling, where they're attached, like prisoners held far too long. But they don't.

I pump the bellows, and Georgia and Micah take all our bags out to the wagon. I believe they also went out to check on Amos.

Brother Mahoney smiles when the song is finished. "Well done," he says, "You did it more than justice." He looks toward the front of the church. "I'll be out for a minute, but members should begin to drift in, in a little while."

"I'll finish warming up," Nathan says, and I resume my treadling. When Brother Mahoney is gone, I look at Nathan. He plays a few more short songs, the ones that were pointed out to him. When he finishes them with a flutter of notes up the scale, he looks at me. I push the wooden knob into the base wood of the organ, sealing the air from escaping through the pipes.

"Where did you learn so much about organs?" he asks, tilting his head a bit toward the left.

"It was in a book I read," I say, vaguely and keep treadling, the carpeted treadle whooshing as is tilts from side to side, the waves a ship sits upon.

****

“So, they get to stay inside and we must walk in this awful mist,” Micah says, shaking a strand of hair from his face. Water drips from the fine ends of it, down the bridge of his nose.

“I would guess so,” I say. As we walk to the edge of the clearing, I’m aware that my hand is at my throat, worrying the necklace that Connor gave me. The chain slips through my fingers, slick with water from the dewy mist.

“What’s your necklace?” Micah asks, noticing my habit.

“It’s nothing,” I say, taking it off and holding the chain so he can see the pendant.

“It’s nothing?” he asks. “It’s only nothing if you let it be.” The pendant spins in the faint light coming through the treetops, catching the cracks and splits inside the smooth ball. They throw lighted rainbows over my plain, grey dress.

“I would suppose so,” I say, slipping the necklace back over my head, but our conversation is cut short afore we reach the Clay Curry Band wagon.

“Here,” Micah says, “You check on Amos and I’ll put our bags away.” I nod, walking around to the front of the wagon, hitched at the edge of the clearing. Yesterday, they had propped the wagon up on some stumps so it wouldn’t be tilted in the mud. Amos was tied to a tree not too far away, eating some grass pulled from the clearing floor.

"Good morrow, Amos," I say, "How was your night? All right, I would guess." He looks at me, his lazy brown eyes drifting around my face. I stroke his nose, my hand sticking his wet fur together and leaving streaks. Amos shakes his head, his ears flapping, and resumes eating the green grass. He is such a funny creature. It takes all you got to get him going, but once he starts, he won't slow down. More than once had I almost fallen off the too-slick top of the wagon after we took a corner too fast. I hadn't, though, and I'm getting better with not falling off- I imagine the fall to the ground would be painful. Perhaps almost as painful as being run over by the same wagon. I stifle a grin.

The high, clear sound of the latch closing on the wagon calls me, and I walk back to where Micah is waiting. "Is everything there?" I ask.

We start walking back to the church. "Aye," he says, "I don't think there is anyone else here but us and Brother Mahoney."

"I haven't seen anyone else," I admit, wiping a strand of hair from my eyes. It's drenched with water from this relentless mist. "But Amos doesn't seem too wet," I say, "Though, we'd best dry him off before we start going, or else the harness will rub through his hair and leave sores."

"'Tis true," Micah agrees, holding the side door of the church open for me, hanging onto the curved, brass handle. Nathan isn't playing the organ anymore, but Arlan is still pumping the treadle. It creaks with every tilt, filling the church with the eerie music. Shaking my head, I move to sit next to the stove again, to dry my dripping locks.

Just as I sit down, the main door to the church opens and in comes a woman. She's dressed all in black, with layers of coats and furs. "Oh, hello dearies," she says, "Good morrow."

"Good morrow," Arlan and Micah say back distractedly, still focusing on the organ.

The woman sits in the back row of the church, crossing her hands over her black furs, and looks around the room. "Now, you'll have to forgive me," she says solemnly, "I am getting old- have you been here before?"

Micah sits down next to me on the threadbare carpet. "No, we're just travelers, passing through."

"Well," she says, her face awash with warmth, "We're glad to have you. I'm Mabel, Mabel McCallister."

But, before we had to introduce ourselves, the doors open again and a young family walks in. They sit in the back, along with Mabel McCallister, who happily takes the red-haired baby from the young, red-haired mother.

While the young parents try to keep numerous, toddler-sized children from running up and down the aisles and tearing hymn books open, Micah turns to me. “Are you dry?” he asks, “If you are, we’d be right to sit in one of the benches. It’d certainly draw less attention to us.”

“I am,” I answer. Micah stands to his feet and offers his hand down to me like a proper court gentleman. I accept it, and we sit in the third row back. The toddler-sized children run up and down the aisle, but one particular one stands there, facing us. Facing me. She looks at my hair, piled along my shoulders in it’s loose, falling ringlets, and down at her long auburn locks clutched in her fists almost austerely. It’s an odd look for the child. “Gaia,” the mother says and pulls her away, to sit in their pew in the back row. More families come in, more people, and soon I can’t see the little girl anymore.

And then there’s a cough, and Nathan begins his music. Arlan pumps the bellows, and Brother Gaius Mahoney stands to the side, watching the wonder as people listen to the organ for the first time in a long while. The vibratos of the lows sound loud in the church and threaten to tear us all apart from the inside. After Nathan had played the few hymns Brother Mahoney requested, he closes the dusty covers of the book, setting it down on the front pew as he and Arlan move to sit down next to us.

Brother Mahoney walks up the front, resting his hands on either side of the light wooden pulpit. "Good morrow," he says, smiling wide. "Now wasn't that a lovely way to start this blessed morning?"

The congregation nods with a chorus of 'Amens.'

"Now," Brother Mahoney says, "if you'll just turn your Bibles to the fifth verse of the second chapter…"

And we listen to the sermon lighted by Brother Mahoney. Through the words and the smiles, this church was a nice difference from the ones at the castle. Those are long and drawn out, and the clergymen always use flowery wording that takes both a dictionary and a thesaurus to decipher. At least this one is short and sweet, well received and well appreciated. I see Arlan pull out the quill from his back pocket, fiddling with the tip of the feather as he listens intently to the rolling, thunder-like baritone of Brother Mahoney. Something to do with his hands, I guess. I just let my fingers play with the button sewn into the cushion and shift in the pew to the words spun in the air above me.

When the sermon ends too soon, people start to trickle out, handing casseroles to the young couple. "We should start heading out," Nathan says, turning to us. "If we want to make it to the next day-town, with the roads as they are and whatnot."

Micah slides the hymnbook he was flipping through into the slot on the back of the pew. "We probably ought to," he says, walking to the door, holding it open for Arlan.

Just then, though, I feel a hand on my arm. It's the round face of Brother Mahoney, creases lining the spaces around his emerald eyes and between them. "Darling, before you go, I need to talk to you."

"What is it?" I ask quietly, pulling away and staring at the torn hem of my dress.

"I know you're not Alayna," he says, "I've seen you standing around at the castle, begging your momma to let you play with the drummers." He takes a breath, waiting until we're the only ones in the room, waiting until Micah, Nathan, and Arlan are gone.

"I know who you are; I know your standing."

I look at him, painting my face with confusion and hoping it isn't too much. "I don't know what you're talking about," I say, "I'm just a poor girl, farm bred and on my way to the city."

"That's a lie," Mahoney says, "It's a terrible thing, to lie, but it's worse to lie in church. To a minister."

I can't help but smile. "Oh, alright," I say, "I'm not a farm girl, you're right." I pause, taking a deep breath of the sharp air, "But you won't tell anyone, will you?"

"Tell, I will not, but I will pray for you. Godspeed, young lass. And good luck." Brother Gaius Mahoney opens the oak door for me, watching me as I walk through and to the wagon.

I don't think Brother Mahoney will tell on us. It doesn't seem like it would fit with his character in the slightest. So then, my burning secret is safe for now, at least. A candle among the rain. But, as I cross the clearing, the sun finally having burnt away the mist, all I can think about is getting Janson back.

It fills my mind like a spring, all the thoughts and memories associated with who I think of as my little brother. He was as close to one I ever got, though, and we thought the same way and looked at things the same, through the same lens of realism. We had more in common than me and any of my birth brothers had. All that separated us was royal blood.

I wrap my hands in my skirt. Black thoughts just turn blacker, but idleness does good for a worried heart. That same statement embroidered on a pillowcase, a piece of stitchery. The ride goes fast, and that is a godsend.

Chapter Eleven

The next little day-town we come to is bathed in the golden light of what sun-rays could filter through the leaves. Micah guides Ole Amos to a stop, right outside the dark-eaved building. I know this town- I've read about it. It was a stable, a large one at that, before the Master-house was taken by fire. The count moved out, the stables became an inn, one of the first original day-town buildings.

It is smaller in person.

There is a man outside, barely older than a lad, dark wavy hair falling into his eyes. It looks like the type of hair to always be just slightly too long and always in the way.

Solemnly, the man arranges pink quartz flagstones in the dirt pathway. “Aye, need a room?” he asks, looking up as the wagon nears.

Nathan shakes his head. “Just need to talk to the inn Tender.”

“Aye, that’s me,” the man says, “It’s my inn.” He looks up at us, pushing a strand of hair from his eyes.

“Oh,” Micah says, surprised, “Whatever happened to ole Jeb?” He slides from the front bench of the wagon, his feet hitting the dirt of the road with a thud.

The man straightens up. “Retired,” he says, “Left it to me. I’m Martin Flynn.” Looking at his palms, he wipes the dirt off them and onto his pants before offering his hand to Micah, who shakes it.

“I’m Micah Ward,” Micah says, “This is my brother, Nathan.” Nathan nods at the man, who nods back. “This is Georgia and Arlan.” We nod as well.

“Then,” Flynn says, his brown eyes shining in the sunlight like polished wood. “If you don’t want a room, what do you want?”

“Well, a room, aye,” Nathan offers, “But we’d be willing to work for it.”

“Clay Curry Band?” Martin says, tilting his head and reading the side of the wagon, “Jeb told me about you. Piano still in the back?" He chuckles at this prospect, nudging the flagstone a little to the left with his foot.

"Aye," Nathan says seriously, running a wary hand over his jaw, as though he's waiting for a judge's verdict.

"I'm sorry, mates," Martin says, sticking his hands in his front pockets of his trousers, "I'd let you all play, of course I would, but we've a wedding here tonight."

"A wedding?" Arlan asks, slipping forward on the smooth wagon top.

"Aye, lad," Martin says, the wind ruffling his dark hair. "A wedding. They booked the whole inn yard, told me if I hired it out to anyone, they'd have my head." He lowers his voice, glancing towards the inn, eyes alight. "And, by the looks of that mother-in-law, I would believe it!"

"Guess we'll be paying for our room this time around," I say, adjusting my skirts to slide to the ground as well.

"No," Martin says, "That doesn't mean you can't work for your room. You just can't play."

"Well, what do you have in mind?" asks Nathan.

Martin bends to adjust another flagstone, burying the edges in the soft dirt. "Besides moving these rocks? There's a platform in the back, in the stables. That needs to be brought out, and 'woody things' brought in to decorate it."

"Woody things?" Micah asks, frowning.

"Aye," Martin says, brushing dark hair away from dark eyes once more. "That's what the bride requested."

"Woody things," Micah nods to himself, his eyebrows knitting together.

"The stables," Martin restates, walking over to a small pile of flagstones by the front door of the inn and picking one up, "the doors are unlocked. In the back."

"When's the wedding?" I ask.

Martin unbends. "What time is it now?" he asks, holding up a thumb to block the sun and extending his littlest finger to measure the distance from it to the trees. "Hour of eleven?"

"Ten?" Guesses Micah, doing the same gesture.

"Well, whatever time it is, the wedding will be soon," Martin says, digging a place for the newest flagstone a few feet down from the previous stone. "Too soon, if you ask me."

"The door is unlocked?" Nathan asks, leading Amos to the tree line and tying him up to the thick trunk of a dire tree. The rest of us slide off the wagon top; I feel the shock travel up the bones in my legs like ripples in water. It still hasn't worn off, even this far into our trip, the hundred times I've jumped down and climbed up.

"Aye, it's open," Martin calls over his shoulder, "Lock broke off past -what?- three years ago, haven't fixed it yet. Not got the time." He brushes a lock of hair out of his face, and bends to pick up a spade, to flatten the ground under another flagstone.

The stable is tucked in the edge of the clearing, the front wall flush with the tree line. Boards cover the front, greyed and shrunken with age, so much so that you can see the inside of the shed at some parts. The door almost falls off its hinges when Micah moves it, and it's dark and damp inside, but the platform Martin was talking about is located easily enough. Close to the middle of the room, it's made out of what seems to be the same material as the walls- rough and course gray wood, so contorted with rain water it might as well have been soaked in the sea.

"You want to grab that side?" Micah asks, gesturing to Arlan and Nathan. Nathan grabs a flatside, while Micah and Nathan take hold of two of the corners. I hold back the door, set to slide over the opening on bars. It seems that the left of the building has sunken into the rich, brown earth, leaving the door always threatening to close violently.

"Georgia," Arlan says, "Go find Martin, ask him where he wants it." I nod, running towards where we came. Martin is still burying flagstones out in the front of the building.

"Where do you want the platform?" I ask. His dark eyes start when he looks up.

"Somewhere out back," he says, nodding a head towards the house building, "By the tree line." I nod, and gather my skirts around me again, so I can run better. "And don't forget," I hear him call after me, "Woody things! To decorate!"

"Nathan," I say, turning the corner of the house, "He wants it out back. Along the tree line."

They had set the small platform down on the ground, held upright on its side by Arlan and Micah, stationed one on each side. "Where along there?" Nathan asked, looking toward the place where the trees meet the clearing.

"Somewhere."

"Aye, boys, let's lift. Out here, let me lead," Nathan says. He lifts the flatside, and the others take the corners, and they carry it a ways, down the tree line. The green, green grass of the clearing slopes down just enough, but not too much, and the platform fits just right at the bottom.

"Aye," I say, picking some leaves off the side of the raised platform, "Now for woody things."

"What is qualified as a woody thing?" Micah asks, glancing at the woods behind us.

"Not a lad knows," Nathan said, "This is a wedding, woman's work." Slowly, almost congruently, they all turn and look at me.

"I don't know," I say, glancing at the surrounding woods in bewilderment, "This isn't a royal wedding. I suppose we're just supposed to go into the woods and find pretty things to bring back?"

The males seem to take this as an acceptable answer, and they head into the heat of the woods, picking paths where the brambles are thinnest. The barbs catch on the thin lace of my underdress, pulling at it, but I'm distracted yet already by the forest. It looks different here. There isn't any color deep in the forest, away from the path. Everything is just shades of brown or grey. Except right there, growing in between a log and the base of a tree, is a small white flower. I bend over and grasp it, where the stem meets the soft bark of the log, and pull. The thin green easily snaps, and I bring it up towards my face. The white blossom is made of six delicate, gently curving petals around a few stalks of yellow center, forming almost two blooms. The whole bud is smaller than the thickness of my thumb.

"Georgia's found a flower," I hear Micah say behind me, his voice muffled by the leaves of the trees around us, "Butterfly blossom, no doubt."

"Butterfly Blossoms?" Arlan asks, picking his way through the green-brown of the brambles towards me. "Is that what they're called? They grew along the water in Jasmine Jewel."

I look at him, his green eyes full of wonder. "Did they?"

"Aye," he says, "but I read that they grow in strands. Too many on the banks of the river to tell back in Jasmine Jewel, but…" he raises his green eyes to look around at the surroundings. There's a pause.

"Ah, there." He points. A white flower grows just a few feet away, edging its way through the damp leaves.

From that flower, we see its companion, nestled a few feet away, between the bramble bushes. The thin white blossom is poking up through the damp, black leaves of the forest floor. It's like this that Arlan and I collect a bouquet of thin Butterfly Blossoms, the blooms spilling over my hands as I carry them through the brambles. We follow the strands of flowers until we've collected more than one fistful, then make our way back through the beaten bramble path we've trampled.

"Georgia," I hear Micah say, but it's muffled. The Ward brothers strayed behind, looking for another strand of Butterfly Blossoms. There's a crashing sound, I turn to see Micah and Nathan tearing through the trees, the brambles clinging for dear life to Micah's trousers.

"Did you find any?" I ask, but his hands are empty and brushing the damp from the woods onto the dark material of his trousers.

"No," he replies, running his hand over his curly mop of hair, "No, I didn't. All we need are flowers?"

I look around. There's no color here, in the forest. If only we were back in Jade City, with the kaleidoscope of wildflower fields that grew there, then we would have many different colors, many different types of blooms to choose from. Here, we've only the white ones. "We should have more to decorate the platform, more than just this bunch of flowers."

"Then what?" asks Nathan, reaching into his pockets for a kerchief to stem a spot of bramble-caused blood. "Everything here is brown."

"Cut some of the greenwood branches," I say to Micah and Nathan, "We'll lay them at the base of the front of the platform. Keep the leaves on them for the green." Micah nods, reaching into his pocket for a small knife. He turns to the closest tree, sawing through the wiry branch with the small knife. It bends to his cutting, and the long branch tips till the leaf-laden end touches the ground. With a small sound, something like a sigh, the branch snaps where it meets the tree.

I pick my way across the thick forest, following the trail of broken branches and trampled leaves that lead towards the inn. The way the forest exists, with its thick trees, is that I can't see the inn and I'm only blindly following the trail we've left. Perhaps only the appearance of trail. But, when Arlan and I break through the last barrier of foliage, we've stumbled out close to the road leading in to the day-town clearing.

"Hiya!" shouts Martin, still arranging flagstones. The pink quartz trail leads from the front door of the inn around back, but we can't see where it goes.

"Hello!" shouts Arlan back, pulling a strand of his hair out of the forest, where it is ensnared in the brambles.

"Have you got woody things?" Martin says, coming closer. He wipes his hands on the thighs of his pants, leaving streaks of dry dirt on them. "I see only the flowers."

"Aye," Arlan says, "The Wards are still in there, gathering branches and such."

"As long as they help me be finished by time of the wedding," Martin says, opening his mouth to say more, but just then the door to the inn bursts open with such a force, it leaves dents in the worn wood siding.

"Martin," demands the lady from the door, "Martin, I need help."

"Help with what?" he asks, turning and tilting his head to the side.

"Girl!" she shouts, ignoring Martin. "Have you time? Time to help prepare the bride for the wedding?"

"Aye," I say, walking towards the door at Martin's insistent nudge. "But I've no idea what's to be done."

"Really?" the lady asks studying me, "Are you not married yet?" I shake my head, and duck it, and hope she moves on to the next subject as I walk into the darkened main room of the day-town inn.

The inn itself is rather large, for ones we've stayed at afore. The main room is large, wood paneled on the sides, heavy tables in the center and halls leading outward. "The bride, Aelyn, is in her room, putting on the dress. I'm Alice, the groom's mother."

"I'm Georgia," I say, quietly, looking at my shoes and praying she doesn't recognize me.

"Well, then, Georgia, do you know how to fasten stays?" Alice asks, "Aelyn bought a dress from a tailor in the city, and we've never had to fasten them before."

"Stays?" I ask, searching my brain for an excuse, "Aye ma'am, my… mistress… lived in the cities."

"So you've seen these infernal devices before?" Alice asks, not waiting for an answer before swinging open the oaken door to the first room on the right. The bride inside is a beautiful, foreign beauty, pale skin and fiery hair.

"Good morrow," Aelyn says, clutching the dress up around her. "Who're you?"

"Aelyn," Alice says, "This is Georgia, she's here to ready you."

"Nice to meet you, Georgia," Aelyn says, turning so her back is to me. "Now, can you tie stays?"

"Aye," I say, dipping my head toward the floor. The dress the bride is wearing is long and white, tight around the stomach, but with area enough under the skirt for a petticoat and ruffles. "Have you a petticoat? You must put the petticoat on underneath, before the stays, or else it won't fit."

"Petticoat?" Aelyn says, "I bought no petticoat. The dress was expensive enough as it is."

"Underskirt, then?"

"No, please, just tie the stays." That was Alice. She pulls at the long, white ribbons stitched at the bottom of the v-shaped slit in the back of the dress, motioning at me. I thread them, keeping them taught as I lace them through the hemp-string loops.

"Is that all?" Aelyn asks, still holding the front of her dress up, though it has little lace cap-sleeves.

"No," I say, and begin looping it through the second row of loops, down to the bottom. "Suck in your breath."

Aelyn does as I ask, and I begin pulling the stays, tight, smoothing the panels off to the sides as I go, just like the maids used to do back home.

"I can't breathe," Aelyn whispers, "I can't go on like this."

"Aelyn," Alice says, "Aelyn, don't you want a tiny waist?"

"Not if I'm going to pass out!" Aelyn says, reaching back to pull the bow, pull the knot and undo it.

"Aelyn," Alice says, grasping her wrist. "You look so lovely with a tiny waist." But Aelyn pulls her hand away, trying again to grab the ribbon. Her fingers miss the white ribbon, once, twice… I grab the strand, and with a slip of the satin ribbon, the knot undoes and begins to loosen the two rows of tightly wound stays.

"I can breathe," Aelyn sighs, more to herself than to anyone else. "Just tighten it enough so it stays up."

"Yes," I say, and set again to tighten the stays, not too tight, but just enough to keep everything in. The white ribbon pulls at the hemp loops, crossing into a pretty zigzag, prettier now that the ribbon isn't strained to keep what wasn't there, in. While I work on this, Alice sets about the finishing touches on Aelyn's hair- little white silken butterflies, to stand out among the red-gold strands. But, besides the pins to keep the butterflies in, her hair is long and flowing, down her back, tucking under just above the stays. The ends of her auburn locks curl just enough.

"Is this right?" I ask her, tying the bow at the bottom and arranging the ribbon ends so that they're hidden within the tulleing of the skirt.

"Lovely," Aelyn says, looking at the mirror affixed to the wall, clouded with age spots and crossed with hair cracks.

The mother-in-law looks to me. "Help her with her shoes," she says, pointing to a pair of incredibly tiny white Mary-Janes by the door.

"Alice," Aelyn says kindly, "This isn't a city wedding. A city dress, aye, but not a city wedding." She addresses me, turning, "No shoes, thank you."

There's a knock on the door. A woman I don't know sticks her head through the door. "Alice, he's here. Waiting downstairs."

Aelyn's face cracks with a wide smile, her straight teeth showing white against her pale skin.

"I'm ready," she says, and Alice hands her a bouquet of wheat-flowers. The space in between the small, straw-colored blossoms is filled with the coarse strings of real wheat. I ponder this- nothing is ever used in weddings I have witnessed except white lilies, traditional and 'pure.'

"Georgia," Aelyn says, pulling up the front of her skirts and walking to the door, "Thank you for fastening the stays. Come down to the wedding, won't you?"

I nod, "Of course."

"Good," she says, taking the arm of someone I don't know, who's waiting right outside the thin door of the room. Her skirts trail just behind her, highlighting her bare heels as they poke out of the lace dress-skirt with every step.

I follow Alice and the other woman out the door, into the lobby of the Inn. There, Aelyn is standing, and a man is affixing a gauzy, lacy veil to the crown of her head, covering her face. I wouldn't suspect he's her husband, he's far too old. Mayhap her father.

The man throws open the inn door with grandeur, letting in light and breeze. On the wind, the light strains of a piano waft in, and everyone stops to notice.

"Go, child," Alice says, pointing me around the inn, "Go sit. The wedding will begin soon." I duck my head in obedience, hoisting my blue skirts round my knees and turning the corner of the inn.

The yard out back is beautiful. While I was helping the bride with her fancy dress, guests have arrived, setting up soft woven blankets in the grass on the ground. The blankets have bright colors and patterns, shades of blue and red and orange that stand out against the green, green grass. The blankets and the people have arranged themselves to form makeshift rows, but they aren't severe. Sometimes guests just show and place their rug off to the side, lying in the sunshine. They sit, with their bare feet crossed in front of them and their backs against the ground, listening to the tunes cascading out of the Clay Curry Piano, set in the back.

Nobody turns to face me as I scan the backs of the people to find the loose, bishop's shirt that belongs to Arlan. He's set a little ahead of the wagon, sitting in the back rows of the guests. He lies atop a light blue rug, just a tinge darker than the skirts draped around my waist. His eyes raise as I get near, round as ever.

"Arlan?" I say, folding my legs underneath me, my eyes lighting around the people. "What's that?"

He sits up, turning to see where I look. In the back of the aisle is a glass jar set on a squat three-legged stool. When guests arrive, they stick their hands in their pockets, pulling out whatever spare money may have found its way there, dropping it into the glass jar with a melodious, light clinking.

"Ah," he says, tipping his chin, "I have read about it. It's a Miran tradition, when guests arrive at a Miran wedding, they empty their pockets into the jar, all the change. Because Miran women get no dowry, this is what the newlyweds get to their name." The sunlight pours over the tops of the trees, flowing through the glass of the jar as a couple drops a few coppers into the top.

I nod. "Where did you get this rug?" I ask Arlan, touching the soft, twisted thread rope fringe.

"Micah pulled it from the back of the wagon." I nod, everything is set in the back of that wagon. It must be bigger on the inside.

I nod once more, but say nothing. Nothing until the piano rings out long, organ-ish tones, and everyone who's been to a forest-people's wedding stand. The bride comes down the slight hill from the other side of the inn, arm linked with the man who affixed the veil to her hair. As they reach the wagon, he lets go of her arm, but she still walks towards the platform we put up earlier. Her feet don't even falter. At the platform up front, the Butterfly Blossom bouquets are mixed with the dark green ferns that grew along the tree line, and affixed to the front of the platform, to decorate it. While I was helping the bride dress, Micah, Nathan, and Arlan arched the tree branches they cut behind the platform, making a lovely, leafy backdrop to the whole thing. Someone- Arlan I would suspect- even decorated them with more Dutchman's breeches, tucked into the dark green diamond-shaped leaves.

"You did well with the decorating," I whisper to Arlan as the bride mounts the platform, and everyone sits back down.

"It wasn't me, 'twas the bridesmaids," Arlan whispers back, folding his legs underneath him once more and resting his chin in his hands.

The wedding ceremony isn't long, not like the three-hour ceremonies common in the city, between two people of standing or what have you. It is a sweet ritual, somehow made sweeter with the lack of overbearing formalities to weigh everything down. When it is over, the people all gather up their rugs, some taking them as they traveled back to their rooms in the inn, others laying them down besides the almost full jar of change and leaving them behind.

"Georgia," someone says, coming up behind us, "Arlan, Nathan, Micah." It's Martin, pushing his hair out of his face. "It seems I've made a grave mistake."

"Aye?" asks Nathan, rubbing his jaw, "And what might that be?"

"With this whole wedding going on… you see, I'm not too great at keeping numbers…"

"Martin."

He sighs, sticking his hands in his pockets apologetically. "You've no room."

"Martin," Micah says, his eyes bending with hurt, and concern. "We've no room?"

"Aye," he says, ruffling his hair and staring at his shoes. "I'm sorry, really, I am, after all you've done to prepare for this wedding as well."

Nathan sighs, rubbing a hand across his jaw and up his face, "We'll sleep out here. What else have we to do?"

"I'm sorry," Martin says, "But hey, when you come back, free room. You don't even have to play. Just come through." He spreads his hands wide with the emphasis of what he's saying.

"Aye, Martin," Nathan says, "Go attend to your guests. We'll lay out here, it should be a nice night anyway." He looks up, as if he is examining the sky's weather, like it isn't already dark out.

With a sheepish, sideways grin, Martin shakes Micah's hand and moves back towards the inn.

****

Chapter Twelve

Nathan kneels off to the side, coaxing a small coal-fire to life. The night was warm enough to not freeze, but not enough for comfort. Certainly not warm enough to go without fire. I watch the sparks catch the starters between Nathan's hands, but soon, they spread to the sticks on the outside. As they quickly burn through the small twigs and stuffing, Nathan puts on more and more wood, breathing onto the tinder, until it's bright enough to keep.

"What are you doing?" I ask Micah, who is sitting on the ground, leaning against the wagon wheel. Draped across his lap is his oddly large fiddle contraption.

"Restringing it," he says, leaning over and biting through a copper toned wire and wincing at the taste.

"What is it?" I ask him, sliding off the driver's bench to sit next to him.

"This?" he asks, turning it over so I can see. "I don't know. It sounds good, that's all I can say for it. It came with the wagon." He gestures towards the wagon with his chin, wrapping another wire around another knob and twisting it, tightening it.

"Aye," I say, nodding. Micah bites through another wire, grimacing.

"It takes guitar wires, though, but only four of them, top four," Micah says, handing the severed wire stub to me. I wrap it around my fingers, pulling a tight knot to keep it in place. Tenderly, Micah stretches the leather strap across the neck of the instrument, setting it beside him. He picks up the fiddle between us and begins to loosen the strings on it, too.

"Restringing it?" I ask.

"Aye, lad," he says, handing me the worn wire and pulling a spare from his shirt pocket. I watch him as he gingerly pokes it through the knob on the head of the fiddle, hooking it in place, and tuning it to the odd half-guitar. I think to myself how it's a world of a lot more complicated than playing the drum. At least with drums, there's only one note to focus on, not however many can be played on this fiddle.

After Micah has packed away his instruments, Nathan tells us, in his gruff voice, that we'd really be waking with the sun, out in the open, and that we'd ought get to sleep. I laid one thin sheet that we'd brought from the inn across the wood of the Clay-Curry Band wagon top, and Georgia and I sleep on the roof, while the Ward brothers slept on the cool, damp grass. As we set it, the wagon rests near the edge of the clearing, and if I turned my head just right, I can see the stars through the thinner parts of the leaves. I think about those leaves.

From what I read, they never do fall, not like the trees back in Jasmine Jewel or even Jade City. The leaves of the Dire Trees turn brown and die, but they don't let go. It's what makes the inner parts of the forest so dark. Sunlight can't filter through. Slowly, my mind turns over the stones, aligning the allegory to people. Some people are so dark, so guarded, because they don't let go of what's died. They clutch the leaves to their trunks, afraid to drop them into the wind. And it makes their life dark.

I listen to the steady breaths of the Ward brothers below us.

"What are you thinking about?" Georgia asks, shifting her arms beneath her head, and leaning it toward me.

"Leaves."

"Leaves?" she asks, "I was thinking about how nice a piece of Cook's cobbler would be right now, but leaves are fine too."

"Yeah," I say, "They just… hang onto the dead ones. It's why it's so dark."

Georgia tilts her head. "Arlan, you're not making any sense."

The air leaks from my lungs. "I know."

Her purple eyes shine in the moonlight, two gleaming gems, and I watch as she closes them, murmuring, "Ok," before she, too, becomes no more than a flurry of sleepy breaths. The light of the moon glints off the bridge of her nose and her flushed cheeks, highlighting them in the night.

The next day is sunny and cool, not unlike the days before it. As always, I am riding atop the Clay Curry Band wagon, but we're not moving. The cracked leather backing of my vinegar-paper journal is open on my lap, almost full with the annotations of our story and its happenings.

"Hey, Arlan, could I get you to drive for a bit?" Nathan asks, turning around in the narrow front seat. Next to Nathan, Georgia is focusing on something in her hands, her poems no doubt, and Micah is asleep below us, in the wagon.

"Drive the wagon?" I ask, looking around. "I've never driven before."

"It's quite easy, you see," Nathan says, holding up the reigns, "Ole Amos knows where to go. Just pull back the straps when he gets going too fast."

"Aye… If you're sure you trust me," I say, slipping across the top of the smooth wooden wagontop and into the driver's bench between Nathan and Georgia. It's a tight squeeze with the four of us in the front- me, Nathan, Georgia, and Georgia's skirts.

"Well, I'm sure you've read about driving wagons," Nathan says, smiling and climbing onto the top of the wagon. He hands me the thick leather chords that control Amos. They're brown and worn, but not cracked, not like old leather is. They're taken care of. I tap the reigns against Amos' sides and he starts to pick up speed, careening around a bend in the path.

Soon, I hear Nathan's deep breaths coinciding with Georgia's quiet ones, reciting poetry to herself. "You know," I say, turning my head slightly to the right, addressing Georgia next to me, "I never would've thought I would ever feel so comfortable around you." I never would have admitted this back at the castle, or even with the soldiers. The solitude of the turning, empty trail must be getting to my head, making me say unexpected things.

"Really?" Georgia asks. I imagine she's looking up from her book, but I can't see her, I'm too afraid to lift my eyes up from the twisting pathway before me. I hear Georgia take a breath. "That's all I wanted. For everyone to see me as an equal. For everyone to feel like…" She stops, her mouth running out of words.

"No, I get you," I say. "Not that I made much of an effort to converse. You know, back at the castle."

I wait for her to say something, but instead I hear her rustling skirts as she adjusts them, turning to face me. The heavy cold-weather skirts add a bustle that I wasn't expecting.

"Really," she says, "You just seemed, I don't know, done with everyone. Quiet. Only interested in your books."

I nod, not knowing what to say. She's right though, and it hurts me just a bit more, down in the pit of my stomach where it used to seem nobody could hurt me. "That's true," I finally say, my voice cracking in the cold air. "I guess I thought they were the only real things that couldn't hurt me."

"You know everything about me," Georgia says, rearranging her skirts again. Her purple eyes study my face. "But I don't know anything about you."

"What, now you're asking?" I say jokingly. I turn to her and feign pain.

"Yes," she replies, mocking me in the same tone.

“Well, I came from Jasmine Jewell,” I say, “My Ma died having me and my Pa died short after. I was cared for by the other street urchins.”

“Who taught you to read then?” Georgia asks, “You knew how when you reached the castle.”

“’Tis true,” I say, “There was this lady, the librarian. She took it upon herself to teach every last one of us how to read and write and be a gentleman. Us orphan children, that is.”

“That must’ve been a daunting task,” Georgia declares, rearranging her skirts once more. The hems keep falling off the edge of the wagon.

“I’m sure it was,” I say, “But I’m grateful because outside of what she taught me, everything I’ve learned, I’ve learned from books.

Georgia smiles, “I could believe it.” She pauses. “Why did you volunteer to be a drummer anyway?”

“So,” I say, instead of answering her, “What are we going to do once we reach Alyak? There’s only one more night of traveling before we get there.”

“Right,” she says, taking a moment to pull her thoughts together, “Would it be better to make a deal? We can’t take her by force, certainly not in her own cave.”

“Not by force? What if we paid some brutes to help us?”

"With the little money we have? We're lucky that the brothers are feeding us as it is!" Georgia says. She sounds exasperated, and I know it's just the fact that we are getting close to Alyak. Close to Thieves' Forest, where Fearless's hideout is rumored.

"Why, you two sound like an old married couple," Micah says, poking his head through the window in the side of the wagon.

"Do we?" Georgia asks, pulling her skirts tighter about her legs. I turn just in time to watch Micah lean out the window to sit on the sill. He waits until we fly around the corner and hauls himself out the window, landing perfectly on the wagon top.

"Something tells me this is not the first time you've done this," Georgia laughs. It's a nice sound, a cascading sound.

"Not at all," he says, voice dripping with sarcasm, "It's too much work to get Ole Amos to stop. Much easier to learn to flip out windows instead."

"I agree," Georgia says, laughing a bit more.

"But what were you saying about people needed to fight Fearless Le Paige?"

"It's just that," I say. "We're not strong enough, and we're not going to just fight her from her own cave."

Micah rests his elbows on his knees. “This is true. It would put us at a disadvantage. But, you did hear about Fearless Le Paige’s background, didn’t you?”

“Of course,” I say.

“You did?” Georgia asks me. “Really? I scoured that library for hours and didn’t find a single thing on her. Started to think she was a myth.”

“She’s most certainly not a myth,” Nathan says, sitting up and running a hand through his wavy locks. “So much is sleep with you three talking so loud. Besides, this forest is full of informants to Fearless. Quiet your voices.”

“What’s her story, then?” Georgia asks, a little impatient.

“Well, it’s a patchwork one, at best,” Micah says, gesturing for his brother to tell the story.

“She was a diplomat, long ago. When I was a boy. I remember the stories that got passed around. Anyway, diplomat. To Mira.” Nathan says, “Then something happened. Nobody really knows what, but she switched sides. She worked as a spy for Mira for quite some time before she was found out. Then, she started kidnapping people, holding them for ransom, just enough money to squeak a living. But, your friend Jansen was the first in a long time… and by far the youngest I’ve ever heard of.”

"Why would she kidnap Jansen?" Micah asks, "She usually held people who were related to the king's work, somehow. But Jansen could hardly be that old."

"I don't know," I say. "I woke up, found the ring. I knew it was Fearless Le Paige as soon as I saw it. She's the only criminal who leaves diamonds instead of taking them."

"Well, she only worked diplomat ransoms, unless she moved to kidnapping just for money," Nathan says. "Did Jansen have any money?"

"No," I say, "None. All drummers are penniless orphans; everyone knows that."

"Then it must be for knowledge," Georgia states, looking at me. Her big purple eyes shine in the green light from above. "You were around him longer than I was. What did he know?"

"Nothing about music," I say, "that's for sure."

"That's not what I meant," she says. "Did you find out anything about his life back at… where ever it is called?"

"Jasmine Jewell," I say, "And not much. He did say that his parents were bookkeepers."

"Well, that doesn't help a whole awful lot, does it?" Georgia asks. She rests her hands in her chin and closes her purple eyes.

"No, you don't get it," I say, easing the reigns, "There are no bookkeepers in Jasmine Jewell. Not as long as I was there. There was no need- especially for the King's retired bookkeepers. Everyone in Jasmine Jewell keeps their own numbers."

"The king's retired bookkeepers?" Nathan asks, "What numbers did they keep?"

"I don't know," I say, "Jansen wouldn't tell me."

"That's gotten us as far as it will," Micah says, "But how will you get her?"

"Get Fearless?" Nathan asks, "You want to get Fearless? I thought you just wanted to rescue your friend. A little distract and run thing.

"We do," Georgia says, turning back to look at him. "We just want Jansen. How will we do it, though? If we *don't* take down Fearless?"

"I don't know," I say, laying the reigns against Amos's side, "I just don't know."

****

The further in the journey we go, the more I'm beginning to see the similarities poke out. Every turn seems to be the same, every tree as well, every rock and every ash pile was one the same. It is as if we had passed the same backdrop an eternal amount of times, just waiting to get to the end.

The last day-town in the Dire Forest could have been any of the others along the trail, though it is probably the largest of all of the inns in the trail… well, maybe not. The rooms are off to the left of the lobby, but it didn't have a piano in the commons room. That means another outdoor concert, complete with jovial dancing tunes performed by Nathan, Micah pulling out strange instrument after strange instrument from the back of the wagon, and Arlan trying to keep up with his 'fast as lightning' drumsticks later tonight.

But, at least the tender in this one is nice and the rooms smells like water and not ale.

"Tonight's our last night," Nathan says, standing next to the stove. "In the Dire Forest that is." We're all positioned around the room, waiting for the ancient clock on the wall to tick down to an appropriate time so we can begin playing and serving.

"Ah, it is," Micah says, ceremoniously, "And you've been with us for so long. We've made enough money with Georgia serving to send back dresses for Alayna and Rosalind. And for that, I must thank you." He nods his head towards the ground, causing his dark curls to flop into his face.

"It wasn't anything spectacular," I say to the brothers, "I just wonder how you aren't performing in concert halls and opera houses across the entire country."

"There aren't many people out there who would rather see us and our strange music than an opera," Nathan says, sitting at the table provided, a rare occurrence.

"I would beg to disagree," I say, sitting down on one of the cots, shoved off to the side to make room for the table.

"Whether you disagree or not," Micah says, standing and glaring at his brother, "We would like to show you something."

"It's sort of a… a tradition of sorts," Nathan says, moving to the window and pushing the shutters outward. They let in a gust of chilled evening air. "You see, we always play at this particular day-town before we reach Alyak and, well, this is the only inn with decorative molding on the outside."

"What do you mean?" I ask as Nathan stands on the window sill, hauling himself outward and upward. His feet stick down from the outside of the inn, splaying outward. I stick my head out the window, into the night, and look up. Nathan is climbing the oaken molding to the roof.

"Go ahead," Micah says, coming up behind me. "Don't fall, but I wouldn't expect you to."

I reach up and grab the decorative curl and tug on it. I find that it's well attached, and so I stand on the wooden sill, clinging to the outside of the building. I jump a bit, but only to catch the lower curl of a vine and leaf. If I prop my foot on this bunch of grapes here, I can just reach the lower rim of the roof.

The grapes seem secure under my feet, I stretch to the overhang of the wooden shingles.

But I miss.

All those nights playing ball and climbing trees, I still can't climb to the roof. My fingertips start to burn as I hang from them, only my one hand hanging on the leaf, but to my horror, the wood starts to peel from the wall. The pins are coming out and I'm going to fall, fall the three stories to the cold ground below. The wind blows through my hair and seems to speed the prying of the leaf. My other hand is searching for a handhold, but there is none. I'm going to fall.

The air blows stronger as the leaves finally give way, and I feel my skirts raise as I begin to fall. My eyes are closed and my arms outstretched, and it feels as if time is slowing. I feel the fingers of a strong, calloused hand grab my wrist and haul me over the rough shingles that tear at the dress hems, and onto the roof.

“Nathan, you just saved my life,” I say, breathless. My face is mere inches from the moss stained shingles, but I’m still unable to open my eyes, scarcely able to even breathe.

After I finally convince my lungs to breath again, to take in air, I sit up on my skirts, brush the now damp hair out my face, and open my eyes.

“It was nothing,” he says, looking at his hands and at me, “I just happened to be in the right place at the right time.” Far below us, I hear Arlan and Micah’s voices echoing off the side, discussing the best way to approach the climb, since I pulled the leaf and the most valuable handhold from the wall. When Nathan grabbed my wrist and saved my life, the leaf fell down to the sunbaked dirt down below us.

I lean back on my heels, curling my legs off to the side. “Are you going to help us rescue Janson?”

Nathan looks down at his hands. “Of course.”

“Alright,” I say, “Thank you. Well, then, why are you helping us rescue Jansen?”

Nathan raises his eyes to the blue sky, his chin in his hand, propping his arm on his knees and looking out over the tops of the trees. “No, tell me this first, why are you trying to rescue Janson?”

“Because no one else will,” I say, picking a dire leaf from the stained shingles and playing with it. It’s velvety greenness bleeds onto my hands, but I wipe them off on the stained apron tied around my waist. "He was like my brother. I have quite a lot of them, you know."

"I know."

"I wasn't just going to write him off. My real elder brothers don't care about talking to me or anything, they cared just enough to keep me from getting hurt playing ball, but that's it. Jansen showed up and he became my brother."

"Is that all the reason?"

"Maybe," I say, wringing my hands, "But I also suppose that there's a second part of it." Nathan looks up, his dark eyes meeting mine. I continue, "I also think that I'm doing this to escape from the castle. It's as if, I don't know, I'm stuck there, *stuck* in the role they've given me."

I pause. "Here, with you guys, I'm free."

"I understand," Nathan says, turning his head, allowing a few moments for my statement to sink in. "But why is Arlan going?"

"I guess it's the same for him. Baby brother kind of thing. They do have a similar story, you know, coming from the same town and all."

"Do they?" Nathan asks, pausing a second and rubbing the stubble on his chin. "Well, to answer your question, I guess then we're helping you for a couple of reasons. Firstly, because it's the right thing to do. Secondly, because you're the princess, and if you were to get hurt, then…" He trails off. I look at my hands once more, my eyes finding patterns in the dire leaf juice spilt there.

Suddenly, Micah hauls himself, panting, onto the roof. He came up over the ledge a few feet further down, like he traveled horizontally along the vine molding. He probably did. Almost as soon as he's fully on the dire-leaf covered roof, he reaches over the edge and pulls Arlan onto the oaken planks. As Arlan makes it over the cantilevered edge, his feet kick the air before catching purchase, throwing him onto the roof as well. They sit there, smiling and breathing heavy before standing and moving down the roof towards us. We sit on the pitched side of the roof like birds, to watch the wagons pull into the clearing, people spilling out of them and pouring into the inn.

I watch a young girl in a purple shift-dress bend over and pluck a yellow weed-flower from the ground. She hands it to a boy, looking a few years older than she, and the boy smells it. He puts it in her hair, takes her hand, and leads her into the inn.

"Travelers," Micah says.

"What?" I ask.

"That girl you were watching? With the yellow weed-flower? Her family are Travelers. They pick up stuff to sell in Alyak, where it's cheaper, and travel across Bora to sell it at a higher price," Micah explains. I notice his hands are stained with the juice from fresh dire leaves as well, leaving the finger tips varying shades of greenish-brown, a stained-glass window.

"Do you see Travelers often?" Arlan asks, making note of this in his notebook, now splayed on his lap. His quill and ink are set to lean against his knee.

"No," Nathan says, "The travelers, they're starting to… disappear. It's faster if you ship the goods from here to Jade City or Port Seaglass, and from there to the West Sector of Bora. They're losing their spots in society."

"Where do they go?" I tilt my head and lean forward over the crest of the roof. The wooden planks are splintery with age; I can pull pieces off with my fingers.

"Who knows?" Micah asks with a sigh. "Maybe they settle down, as farmers or what not. Maybe they live in the middle of the Dire Forest, where the trees are the thickest and no one can rob them of their way of life."

I think that over… maybe they live in the middle of the forest. Keeping to themselves. I stand up and look around me. Sitting down, I couldn't see over the tops of the Dire trees, but up here I can see. All I see is trees until the leafy tops meet the silvery mist in the distance, the clouds that drift too low.

The forest spans in every direction, and it's like I'm in the middle of the world, the middle of everything and nothing all at once.

Chapter Thirteen

****

Alyak is like nothing I ever expected. I am used to Jade City, the hum of people talking, vendor keepers shouting their wares. It is crowded there, but nothing could've prepared me for this, not even books. Markets in Alyak are so full of people, you couldn't fit another in, even as early as it is. There are six, seven, eight stalls all in a row, selling the same cloth or the same jewelry, shouting over each other to get their wares sold. People rush all around me, I can't hardly pick one to focus on. A lass rushes past the wagon, sporting loose trousers and eyes rimmed in black. High-born women glide past, their full skirts the biggest I've seen since the palace, and they're bumping into paupers dressed in rags. When we stop to let another wagon pass us, people flood the space between. Some even hop the hitchings securing us to Ole Amos. A little boy, somewhere between poor and poorer, pulls Amos's tail as he walks past. Amos rears, almost landing on a woman walking in front of us, carrying a child. She gapes and hugs the baby to her chest, running to the other side of the narrow street, shouting obscenities all the way.

Slowly inching forward, we make it past the last of the vendor stalls and out of the open-air market. "What do you think we should do now?" Micah asks.

Georgia looks at us, her purple eyes gaping. "We should find where Fearless lives. Her cave, if lore serves correct."

"Where do you suppose we find that? We can't just expect to stumble upon a sign that says, Fearless's Cave, three hours walk south," Nathan breathes out, carefully guiding Ole Amos around the holes carved into the street by wagon wheels.

"No, we will not," Georgia says, giving him a look that serves death. "Maybe people around here know where it is?"

"I don't know," I say, "There isn't much trace of her left, at least not in the books."

"Well, it can't hurt to try," Georgia retorts, rearranging her skirts. They're the fullest ones she has, worn on suggestion by Micah and Nathan. A push to the upper class. If only they saw here closet back home.

"It can hurt," Nathan says, "You've never been to Alyak before. Folks here will as soon kill you as look at you."

"Now, that can't be true," Georgia says. She tucks her necklace into her dress bodice, concealing it, flips her long hair over her shoulders, and slides off the roof of the wagon. Lifting her skirts, she picks her way over to where a young man leans against a vending wall, wavy hair in face, one hand shoved deep in his trouser pocket, the other hooking a jacket over his shoulder.

"Hello," we hear her say over the overwhelming din of the crowd.

"Oh, Lord, this can't be good," Nathan says under his breath, leaning on his knees.

"Hello," the boy says, looking a touch apprehensive. He looks around, trying to see if she belongs to anyone or anything.

Georgia says something to him, but we can't hear it over the rogue screams of a baby somewhere nearby.

A moment later Georgia returns, looking a bit sullen. "You were right," she says, "It was not a good idea to ask people on the street."

She pulls herself onto the wagon roof next to me and crosses her arms over her stomach, folding into herself.

"Well, the only information we'll get is from some poor man who's had too much ale," Nathan says.

"It's only midmorning," I ask, "Where will we find someone drunk at this hour?"

Nathan and Micah make eye contact. "Port Calypso," Micah says, gathering the reigns in.

"The port?" Georgia asks, "I thought it was supposed to be quite lovely."

"It is," Nathan says, raising his eyebrows, "Between the hours of twelve and nine."

Georgia and I don't say anything else, we just watch the buildings drift by. They turn from high end stores to low end stores to houses, and back again. After a while of driving, we can see the river, tucked neatly in between two banks of buildings, edged right up against the cloudy river.

It's a muddy brown-red, with docks sticking out and boats tied up, as haphazard as the vendors at the market. The boats that drift past are only the flat-bottomed river boats that travel up the river and naught but anywhere else. If you want to see big ships, you have to travel to Port Seaglass, the port on the inlet, a week's journey south of here.

Nathan ties Amos to a worn dock post, away from the banks and the docks of the river, away from the people, seamen, rivermen, and tourists all alike, rushing past. Micah hops off the roof, next to me, and moves to help Georgia down with her skirts.

"I can do it myself, thank you very much," she replies, before getting her foot caught in the lace hemline of her skirts and falling to the ground. She lands on the wooden plank roads, but picks herself up and brushes the dirt and who-knows-what-else off her full skirts before acting like nothing ever happened.

"You haven't been here before, right?" Nathan says to me, looking out over the river.

"No," I reply, "not before now."

"Well, that river there? It's the Borian river on this side, but if you go to Mira, over there, it's the Miran river."

"What?" Georgia laughs, "How can that be?"

"Both countries wanted it named after themselves," Nathan shrugs, "Refuse to address it otherwise." An old man walks by, lugging a rope laden with fish. "That's just the way it's always been."

The old man turns around and drags the fish back where he came, face sullen and weathered to gray. We all watch him leave before talking again. "How will we find someone to talk to?" Georgia asks.

"We find the nearest tavern house," Nathan says. "We're at the end of the port now, we'll just walk up that way." He gestures with his chin to the upper part of the boardwalk. Far up, I can see people milling about, a mix of tourists, fisherman, and deckhands. We start walking, and I watch my feet to avoid planks broken through from years of weather, just waiting to trap any passerby's foot. The cracks between the rotting dark colored wood are filled in with sand and dirt, growing along the edges are grass and yellow weed-flowers. The first building we pass is a fish shop, the paint worn off the wood, turned grey with age and weather. People drift by, peering into shop windows and shopping. Deckmaids walk quickly past in their unfilled skirts, hoping to pick up all they need before they must report back to the riverboats, tied up at the piers along the side of the boardwalk.

"Here's a tavern house," Micah says, pushing open the door. The small shack contains more people than I thought it would at this hour. A ragged deckhand drifts in, pushing his way around us and to the bar, where he orders an ale and talks drunkenly to the man next to him.

Here, inside the bar, men sit at the round, wooden, ale-washed tables all around. Some lie, passed out, unmoving, but those who are moving are either on their first ale or their thirtieth. There's no in-between.

Nathan directs us to an empty table in the corner. “Stay here, I’ll see what I can find.” He moves to the bar, sitting a couple of stools away from a clearly intoxicated fisherman. He orders something from the Tender girl, who’s not wearing near enough clothing, before leaning over and commenting something to the fisherman. The drunk fisherman laughs in agreement before taking another swig of his drink. Nathan moves over a chair, closer to the deck hand and they start talking, voices low.

“You here for anything?” the Tender girl says, resting her hand on the back of Micah’s chair.

“No, we’re just… waiting for someone,” Georgia says dismissively.

“Suit yourself,” she says, going behind the bar. I go back to watching Nathan and the fisherman talk. Abruptly, the fisherman stands up, swaying as he struggles to keep the ground below him.

“Look, I don’t know who you are, but don’t ever talk to me again,” he slurs, stumbling out the door and onto the street. I watch his shadows pass by through the oil paper windows.

Nathan drops a few coins on the counter afore coming over to us at our table. “Well, that didn’t go as planned.”

Micah runs a hand through his hair, “Apparently not.”

"Shall we try another bar?" Nathan asks, raising his eyebrows a bit.

"Sure. Just let me try this time."

****

Three hours later, and we are running out of bars. In fact, this is our last one, the last shack stationed on the crowded strip of Port Calypso. At all the other bars, we were either shouted at till we left or the Tenders kicked us out. None of them gave us reasons or warnings, though, so at least we were on the right track. At least, that's how we comforted ourselves.

This bar has thin walls that tilted too far to the left and a battered sign hanging over the door that read 'River's' in sloppy, kiltered Miran. It's much the same thing we've seen since the first tavern by the river. Dim light coming in through oil paper windows highlights the several drunks in the room. The air smells of unwashed people and strong ale, and Micah, Arlan, and I are ushered to a small table in the corner. The same routine.

Nathan sits at the bar, orders cheap ale he won't drink a sip of, and strikes up a conversation with the man next to him. It's late and the bars are emptying out, so there's less people to talk around us. Less bits of conversation to pick out among the rest of them. I can at least make out what Nathan is saying.

"Are you a deckhand here?" he asks, pretending to take a swig of ale.

"Nah," the man says, his words sloshing together like the strong ale in his mug. "Who're you?"

"I'm just passing through," Nathan replies. The man laughs hard, like Nathan made a joke, but he didn't. He takes hold of his glass, draining all but the last bit.

"I heard that you're the man to talk to when you want to know something about someone," Micah says to the man, dropping his head like he's about to hear a secret.

"Yeah, that's me," the man says, his head lolling around his shoulders before coming to rest on his hand. The bartender comes over, and the man stares at his refilled ale before deciding to take another drink. "How many people do you want to know about?"

Nathan leans in closer. "Just one… Fearless Le Paige?"

The man is taken aback. He leans in a little closer, his muddy eyes blinking glassily. "Look mister, I dunno who you think you are, but we don't talk about… her… around here."

He pauses a moment. "I gotta go." He stands, knocking the sad-looking bar stool over and stumbling out the oil-papered door.

Just then an old lady approaches us, seeming to come from nowhere, appearing out of thin air. “Good morrow,” she greets us, dipping her greyed head, “I heard you were looking for someone.”

“Did you now?” Micah asks, leaning in on his elbows. “Who are we looking for?”

The old lady just looks at him before crossing her hands over her stained blue pinafore dress. “I just thought you would like to know, lad, that you’ll find her *elyasiba et bocaj asil.*”

“What?” Arlan asks, “What does that mean?”

“You’ll figure it out. Eventually,” the old lady says, pushing a tendril of grey hair from her face.

“Who are you?” I ask.

“*Ekule*. Nobody,” she says, pulling her woolen shawl around her, draping herself in gray and solemnly walking toward the door.

“What was that about?” Arlan asks, as Nathan pulls a ragtag chair up to the table.

“*Ekule,*” I say. “Nobody.”

“That’s what the lady said,” Arlan says. “What does it mean?”

“Nothing,” I say. They stare back at me with blank eyes. “No, really. It’s Miran for nobody or nothing. What that lady said was in Miran.”

"Do you know Miran?" Nathan asks.

"Yes," I tell him, pulling out my book of sonnets from my sleeve. "I learned it in its entirety a few years ago. Mother says it's diplomatic. Can I borrow your pen?" I ask Arlan.

"Of course," he says, pulling out a pen he whittled from dire wood on the trail after he sharpened the quill to nothing. In scratchy, quillish strokes, I write down what the old lady said on the back inside cover.

"*Elyasiba et bocaj asil. Elyasiba* means, uhh, 'to meet' or 'meeting'. *Et bocaj asil* translates to, directly, 'the gorge, sky.' Whoever that lady was, she said that Fearless's hideout is where the sky meets the gorge."

"Where the sky meets the gorge," Nathan says turning to Micah. "Do you think she means that flooded quarry?"

"What flooded quarry?" Arlan asks.

"A little way from the edge of town is an old marble quarry. It ran out of marble years ago and flooded with the rains," Micah explains.

"If that's the closest gorge, then I would assume that's it," I say.

"How far is it?" Arlan asks.

"Not very," Nathan says, standing up. Reaching over, he hands the bartender a few coins. "Keep the change," he tells her. She smiles and sticks the coins in her apron pocket.

We walk out to the wagon, and I start to pull my skirts around my legs, not knowing how I am going to manage to climb on. "Would you like a hand?" Micah asks, offering his and smiling at the pun, "Seeing as you fell the last time."

Begrudgingly, I take his calloused hand and use it as balance to climb onto the front of the Clay Curry Band wagon. Micah climbs into the wagon next to me and takes up the reigns, tapping them against Amos's back. Almost as begrudgingly, Amos starts forward as Micah guides him onto the streets and toward the edge.

The tree line grows closer, and I can see where the curvy road turns worse. It goes from cobblestone to dirt, and then dirt filled with holes. "Where are you going?" a voice cries out, panicky like.

I look to Micah, but his eyes are already darting around, confused. "Who said that?" Nathan shouts, scanning the tree line as it flashes past.

"Aye, me," the same distressed voice calls out.

"Who?"

"Me, I said, you fool!" Just then, a head pokes up from the back of the wagon. Its hair is light, streaked with dirt and loose leaves. The face that goes with it belongs to a little boy, also streaked with dirt and loose leaves.

"What in the world are you standing on?" Nathan says, looking over the edge and hauling the little boy onto the wagon top behind him. I turn around and cross my arms on the smooth wooden top, to watch what all is going on.

"Naught," the boy answers calmly. "I'm Tad," he announces, after a pause.

"Aye, Tad," Nathan says, his voice crescendoing to a point, "what are you doing hanging onto the lock on our wagon?"

"Warning you," Tad answers, leaning so that his face is but a few inches from Nathan's. "You know what's this way? Death comes to all who travel it." He shrugs. "Least that's what I heard."

"Death?" I ask.

"Aye, miss, death. None ever return." Tad pushes a strand of shaggy, wavy hair from his eyes and leans forward, his fingers wiggling like he's casting a spell.

"Do you know why none return?" Micah asks him, turning around.

"Fearless gets 'em." Tad leans forward, squinting his eyes slightly and smiling.

"Fearless?" Arlan asks, faking astoundment, "Fearless Le Paige? I thought she was just a myth."

"Listen or not," Tad says, "just remember, I warned ye." He swings his legs off the edge of the back of the wagon. "Good luck and brave to you." With that, Tad pushes himself off the speeding wagon, hitting the dirt road and rolling with the force. We just see him stand and wave as we go speeding around the corner.

"Well, that was a bit odd," Nathan says, turning back around and running a hand through his hair. It sticks straight up.

"Leastways, we know we're headed in the right direction," I say, turning around to adjust my skirts, as they had gotton twisted with the whole Tad escapade.

"I wonder why he would tell us the truth about Fearless when all the deckhands and deckmaidens wouldn't," Micah wonders.

"Probably because he's a kid and he doesn't know the taboos," Nathan answers.

"That's true," Arlan responds, pulling out his journal and transcribing the Tad incident. We rush around yet another turn, and I almost fall, but catch hold of the wagon top just in time to save me from the flashing rock path below.

It does jar Arlan, though, causing his pen to race across the face of the journal, leaving a marring trail of ink. Arlan sighs, saying, "I think I should wait until we stop to write."

“Probably a good choice, lad,” Nathan says, and the next so many minutes go by in silence surrounded by the fresh-faced trees. The forest here is different than the dire forest, the trees are father apart and filled in between with many stumps from lumber harvesting. The road is clear of leaves and not carpeted with them, and along the sides grows green grass and other vegetation. In the Dire forest, there isn’t enough light that comes through to support much else than trees and leafless, hitchhiking brambles.

But, up ahead, I see a clearing peeking through the tree line and the curves. Or, not a clearing, rather, the trees just stop. “Is that it?” I ask.

“Aye, lass,” Nathan confirms, straightening up just a bit to see better. “The flooded marble Quarry.”

“Why flooded?” Arlan asks.

“Flooded because it rains, lad. They ran out of marble before I- nay, after I- before Micah was born,” Nathan says, rubbing his chin thoughtfully.

“What shall we do once we get there?” Micah asks, leaning back with the reigns in hand to slow Amos, face marked with worry.

“Once we get there, no, we are there,” Arlan says, quietly, “See the smoke?”

"Aye, I see it. It seems to come straight from the ground," Nathan replies, and it does, mist spewing from the rocky ground like water does in a stream.

"I would bet that Fearless has a cave under the ground. See the door in the cliff? You can see it from here," Arlan says as we come to a stop. And indeed, he was right; hidden in the rock cliff is a door. It is greyed with weather, blending into the ashen grey rock almost perfectly. If we kept going on the road, we'd cross right over it and never look back once.

"Pull the wagon off the trail, Micah," Nathan instructs solemly, dropping his voice a notch. Micah does as he's told, pulling us into a smaller, outcut clearing hidden behind some bushes and trees.

I climb down from the wagon, managing not to snag my skirts this time before setting my feet on the dirt ground.

"Aye, Madge, can't you go any faster?" cries a woman's fierce voice, loud as the wind, as a dark horse comes barreling from nowhere.

Chapter Fourteen

Nathan grabs the back of my dress, hauling me to the ground and out of sight behind the bushes. "Stay here," he breathes afore he pulls himself into a crouch. I turn my head and see Micah and Arlan both lying flat on the ground as well.

"I think whoever that was must've gone," Micah says, "I don't hear horse steps anymore."

"Whoever that was?" I whisper, echoing Micah in surprise, my voice raising. "That was Fearless Le Paige in the flesh!"

"Can you be sure?" Nathan asks, helping me up despite my skirts.

"Aye," I say, "Her long black hair streaming behind her, her black horse. It was her. Who else would be out this far, at this time of day, looking like that?"

"Well, I think it was her as well," Micah lends.

"What shall we do now?" I ask. "Now that Fearless has gone."

"We must make sure there's nobody else watching Janson," Arlan tells us.

"How are we going to do that?" Nathan asks, his voice dripping at the edges with ridicule, "Walk through the door and shout, 'Honey, I'm home?'"

"Don't be like that," I tell him, "I'm sure Arlan has read something."

"Aye, Georgia," he says, quietly, "We listen through the fireplace."

"Sounds good enough to me," Micah says, hooking his thumbs in his suspenders and strolling out onto the street like he does this every day.

"Micah, brother, what are you doing?" Nathan cries, dashing out into the street and grabbing Micah's shoulder.

"Walking," Micah replies, calmly.

"Be quiet," Arlan tells them, stepping onto the road as well. "Maybe there is someone in the cave. They'll hear us and then… then we'll be dead, and this'll all be for naught."

Arlan steps out onto the road, and I follow, hiking my skirts up to avoid scooping dirt in the hem when I step over the ridge. The road here is coated with a fine layer of gravel, courtesy of the quarry. We say nothing, and I concentrate on the crunching that our feet make as we walk. We reach the end of the canyon, and the view is spectacular.

Greyish white rock drops down to a pool of water below, reflecting the sky and the evergreens that grow in the cracks in the rock face. The quarry is slightly rotund, edged in dirt, grass, and dire trees, with a road that travels all the way around, looping back in across the hole from here. The windy road zigzags back and forth and down, eventually leading under the glass smooth surface of the lake below. The point from where we are and the bottom of the clear lake is many leagues, and I can't help but push thoughts of falling from my mind.

A gust of wind catches my loose curls, tossing them across my face and I pull my arms around me, tighter.

Our ragtag group walks the few lengths to where the smoke emerges from the ground. Set in a circle above the door in the rock wall are several stones, three arm lengths from the edge. The smoke is thick near the bottom, white, steam-like smoke. Arlan drops to his knees with a hand on either side of the chimney hole, dropping an ear down to listen.

His face screws with concentration as he listens. Finally, he sits back on his feet. "I don't hear anyone, anyone at all," he says. "Should I say something?"

Micah leans back. "Who's to say she doesn't have backup?"

Nathan's face looks cross. "We would at least hear something then. Maybe Fearless doesn't have Janson here."

"No," I say. They all look at me. "No, that's not right. He has to be here. He just has to be."

"Georgia," Nathan says, reaching out for me, opening his mouth to say more.

"No," I tell him, pulling away, "He's here."

"Georgia," Nathan says, more firmly, but more sad. "I don't think he is."

"Can we at least check?" I plead, quieting my voice that had gotten loud when I wasn't looking. "I'll go in and do it myself, if that's what it comes to."

They all look at me. "I'm going to go."

Arlan looks torn, staring at the ground and scuffing piles of rocks with his shoe edges. He doesn't want to think that Janson's not here. "No," he says, slowly, "No, I'll go in. I'll do it." He rocks back on his heels, hands in pockets, before starting to walk toward the stairs carved in the stone before anyone can reach out and stop him, reach out and catch him.

"I'll go too, then," Nathan says, following him and looking back. Micah starts to go, but Nathan stops him. "You and Georgia go back to the wagon. Look out for Fearless, in case she comes back."

"Are you sure?" Micah asks.

"Yes," Nathan says, patting his brother's shoulder. "We're fine. We'll be out soon, with Janson."

With Janson. I sigh.

Chapter Fifteen

****

We stand at the top of the stairs. They're made out of the same stone that surrounds the rest of the quarry, carved shallow and steep. Fit snugly in the bottom, the door is twisted and oddly shaped, made to fit the opening, nestled in close to a window, made with real glass. The glass has a faint yellow-green tint, meaning it was forged with mountain powder, made to glow after the sun has gone.

The door handle is twisted, weathered bronze, coated in a fine layer of rock powder, perhaps blown in from the quarry. It blends in well with the rest of the door, the rest of the wall. When I grab the handle, dust comes off on my hands, but the door swings well on its hinges. The sight of the inside of the cave is nothing less than what you would expect, but we just stand there, taking all of the oddities in.

The rock-hewn walls are filled with shelves, towered high with books and other odd things. The walls are lined with silver lanterns, filled with slick yellow oil mixed with mountain powder. The mountain power to keep them burning longer, adding just a hint of green to the flame, just enough for the shadows to lie to you. Off to the side stands a worn brick fireplace, double sided and separated with an iron grate.

"Arlan, is that you?" A voice cries hoarsely, in disbelief.

"Janson!" I say, trying to find where the voice is coming from. There are no other doors in here, no windows, just books and journals.

"Here!" Janson shouts, and then coughs. "The shelves!" The voice comes from behind an old wooden bookcase, crowded high with stuff, and pushed behind a table. In-between a the old, leather bound books is a small hole with a face pressed up against it.

I rush to it.

"Janson," I say, straining across the table, "Janson, are you alright?"

He coughs, saying, "I'm not dead, so I've got that going for me." He coughs again, a racking sound that echoes throughout whatever room he's in. "The lock," he gasps.

"I see it," Nathan says, nudging me out of the way and bends to examine the lock. "I've never seen anything like it."

"Aye," Janson says, "Fearless wears the key around her neck."

"I can't break it," Nathan says, "I can't pick it. I don't even know where to start. It's all heavy brass."

"We'll go find her, get it. We'll get you out, I promise," I tell Janson, gripping the shelves for balance.

"Be careful, though," Janson says, his eyes filled with worry… or fear. "She just went out for water."

"Went out for water, come back with company," a female voice says out of nowhere. Standing across the room, behind us, is a woman- Fearless Le Paige. "Mr. Janson, I believe you and I have guests." Janson shrinks away from the window beneath the shelves.

I'm too dumbfounded to speak. She came in without even a sound, not a door squeak, not a door closing, or footsteps. Nothing. Nathan straightens up, showing his hands. "Ma'am," he says, dipping his head, playing formality in the place of fear.

Fearless just stands there, breathing for a second, before crossing the room momentarily. Her arms reach for something on a shelf, something she puts in the insewn pocket in her frock vest, but I can't see it.

While her back is turned, my eyes dart around the room, trying to find some sort of plan. Something, anything. Anything to defeat the futility my mind is trying to tell me is true. All I can think about is how the window is cracked open a little. All I can thing to do is drop something…the lightning bolt drumsticks out, into the quarry, hoping Georgia or Micah will see them. Will see them and come rescue us. With the last thought I can muster, I grab a book from the shelf at random and toss it out as well. I hear them land with the noise of paper on ground outside the window, hoping they didn't fall too far and cascade into the lake.

Fearless strides across the room and back again, her black boots clicking against the floor. "Now, company like this, when the house is a mess," she says, gesturing her wiry arms around her, "I do wish you had given me some kind of warning, though." She walks to the center of the room, still between us and the doorway. Janson is right, though, she does wear the key around her neck. A large brass thing on a chain, it rattles in the space between the buttons on her frock vest.

I look to Nathan, but his eyes are dead focused on Fearless, seemingly watching her as she stands there, hand shoved deep in pocket.

"Now, who are you?" she asks, moving closer, resting her opposite hand on her hip. There, I see, tucked in the deep folds of her vest, is a knife, the handle glinting in the sunlight.

"Just travelers," Nathan says, but his voice wavers.

"Travelers, that come into my house unannounced?" she says, moving closer yet. "No, I don't think that's right."

She looks to me. "You're Arlan, right?" I nod. "Janson would not stop talking about you, about how you were going to come and rescue him."

I say nothing.

She raises her eyebrows, brushing a piece of hair from her face. "He talked of you coming… and a Georgia? Is Georgia around here somewhere?" She feigns looking around, swiveling her head.

"She's not," I say.

Fearless spits out a term that would make any grown man pale, and I want to slap her, I want to rid us of her, but I can't get into a fight. Not with her, I wouldn't win. The pride I swallow tastes bitter, though, as I clench my wrists and try to stop a fight.

"Now, look. You're here. This is such a happy little reunion, isn't it?" she says, shifting her gaze from me to Nathan once more. Fearless pulls the knife from her belt and looks from it to Nathan. "You'll do what I say, right?" The green light from the mountain powdered lanterns glints off the blade, making it long and sharper than I pray it is.

"Never," he replies. To which she nods, like she's thinking it over, sticks the knife back into her belt, and rushes toward him. With one smooth motion, like silk over water, her fist strikes Nathan's throat, sending him backwards, coughing and sputtering. With a sound more like thunder than anything else, he crashes into the tables and knocks things off, before hitting the stone fireplace, hard. Nathan falls to the ground among the broken tchotchkes, still gasping for breath. It's a horrible sound.

"You'll be easier, won't you?" Fearless asks, turning to me, menacingly.

"No," I say back.

"Arlan, don't!" Janson shouts from behind me.

As calm as can be, though, Fearless reaches into the pocket of her sleeveless frock. Running through her fingers are streams of green-yellow powder. She slaps my cheek with her powder covered palm.

The pain is so instant, so intense that I fall backwards, onto the table and then to the hard floor. My own palms can't quell the fire that must be catching on my face. I can feel the distinct outline of her hand, and, and, and I can't think. There are flames on my face. Flames. The floor is far away, though I am sitting on it. Flames. And then, and then, and then…

Silence.

Chapter Sixteen

"Arlan," says a voice. It sounds so far away. "Arlan, you're alright." My eyes are held down with lead weights, I can't move anymore.

I pry them open, but everything is still spinning, a blurred mess of colors.

"Arlan?" asks a different voice. I know this one, I've listened to it and it's stuck somewhere in the back of my mind.

"Nathan?"

"Yes," he says, and I feel hands on my shoulders, picking me up and propping me up. "Arlan, are you alright?"

"I can't see," I say, panicking, lifting my hands to my face. "I can't see!"

"It'll get better in a minute," another voice says. "It always does." A hand pats me on the shoulder and pulls my hands from my face.

Slowly, the colors start to gather themselves together, and my eyes focus. I blink hard. I'm propped against the stone wall, in a room I've never been in before, with Nathan and Janson standing over me, looking concerned.

"Arlan, can you see now?" Janson asks. I blink hard, and there it is. Janson's face.

"Yes," I reply, shifting my gaze. He's a lot skinnier than he was when we were back at the castle. I didn't think that was possible. His hair's shorter, and he's wearing different clothes, but other than that, he's just the same.

"Do you know what happened?" Nathan says, settling himself on the floor next to me. Janson sits in the spindle legged chair in the corner, resting his chin in his hands.

I shake my head, and the effort nearly hurts more than when Fearless hit me.

"Fearless slapped you with mountain powder," Janson says, leaning forward. "The pain knocked you out."

"How… why does it hurt?" I ask, as though I'm in a daze.

"I thought mountain powder just made stuff glow," someone says. Nathan?

Janson shifts in the chair. "Not this kind," he tells me. "This kind is unstable, it… it, uh, burnt your face."

I've lost all the little strength I had, my hand on my cheek. It's like my bones are hollow, and my muscles are stretched out. I can feel, but I can't move and slip down the wall like a stream of water, unable to stop. The stone floor feels cool against the burnt skin on my face.

****

"Do you see that?" Micah asks.

"See what?" I respond, picking up a rock from the ground and worrying it with my fingers.

"That," Micah repeats, drawing out the syllable. He points to the door of the cave. "I swear I saw something."

"What?" I stress again.

"I think…" Micah begins, rolling forward. "I think they're drumsticks."

"Drumsticks?"

"Yeah, sticks. They fell out of the window just now."

I stand up, pulling the skirts out from around my feet. Walking over the cave, quietly, I bend over the edge. He's right. They are Arlan's fast-as-lightning drumsticks, along with a small, leather bound book splayed on the rocks. I motion Micah closer, and he kneels next to me on the slightly damp ground.

A female voice. “Is Georgia around here somewhere?”

“She’s not,” another voice says. Arlan.

The female says something, but I can’t hear it. The rest of the words I can’t hear either, but I know it must be Fearless speaking. The words blur and vary in volume as she walks around the cave.

Micah leans close, his breath moving the hair about my ears. “Fearless?”

I nod, sidling away from the edge, backing -then running- toward the wagon, hidden in the clearing. I press my back against the cool wood of the wagon, leaning against the exposed wheel. When the alarm that rose in my stomach has gone down, I say, “When did she get there?”

“I don’t know,” Micah says, running a hand through his dark curls, his eyes alight with fear. “I didn’t see her go past, and I was watching the whole time.”

“As was I,” I say to him. He’s holding the drumsticks and the journal that had tumbled out the window in shaking hands. He ducked to get them while I was running back, I suppose.

"What do we do now?" Micah asks, sticking the journal and sticks in his back pocket. "I mean, now that Fearless has caught Arlan and Nathan."

"We go to town. We find somewhere to eat. And we gather our wits. I don't know," I tell him after a pause, rubbing my face. "I'm going to change, though. This dress is more harm than good."

Micah nods, and swallows hard. With a click and some hesitancy, he opens the lock to the back of the wagon, handing me my skirt bag from behind the piano. Then, he walks out onto the street, and sits down in the soft grass on the edge, pulling his legs close to him and looking terrified.

Opening the bag, I dig around until I find a soft dress that I got from Rosalind. Walking round to the back of the wagon, I take off the blue silk overdress, and the many layers of petticoat worn under it. The grey dress slides over the linens I am already wearing and I toss my skirt bag onto the top of the wagon.

"Are you ready?" I ask Micah, stepping through the trees and out onto the gravel road.

"Aye," he says, standing up. Now free of my skirts, I climb onto the top of the wagon with ease and pull the skirt bag into my lap. Micah sits on the bench in the front, prying Amos from the greenery that he was munching on. He guides him onto the rough path, coaxing him to full speed, racing so fast, I almost fall off. I grab onto the lip of the wagon top as we swing round a corner and almost tip to our side. This is the fastest we've ever gone.

"It's a wonder you haven't wrecked this thing," I say to Micah as a bump sends us ramping into the sky.

"I was thinking the same!" Micah says back, shifting to absorb another wild swing. The next stretch is straight, past the fields and the trees that break them up. As fast as we're going, we should arrive at town soon.

We reach the edges soon enough, the huts turning to houses, which get closer and closer together until they join and become buildings and that's the city. Sitting between a seamstresses' shop and shoemaker's store sits Tad, scraping something from the bottom of his shoe. "Hey," he shouts, standing up. "You're back!" He jumps up and down, spinning and such.

Micah pulls ole Amos to a stop. "Indeed."

"But where's the other two? The other man and the boy?"

"Fearless took 'em," Micah tells him.

"I told ye," Tad shouts, pointing a finger. "I told ye, I told ye!" He hops up and down, bouncing around and dancing to the chant. "I told ye, I told ye!"

“Lovely child,” I murmur to Micah as he gets ole Amos going again, leaving Tad behind, dancing in the street.

We bump from the dirt path and onto the cobblestones of the main street, and, just like before, people wash around us like laundry water. A lady with a wide, red skirt and red bonnet walks alongside a man in a yellow three-piece suit. Street children run along, ducking about skirts and picking bread from baskets carried by dames not paying enough thought. A rough looking deckmaiden carries a child down the street, both barefoot and crying.

“Where do we go?” I ask Micah.

“Anywhere we can,” he replies, gripping the reins and leaning forward.

We end up behind a somewhat suitable tavern-hotel. The wooden siding is peeling from the beams they’re attached to, bowing outward. Chipped paint and cracked windows complete the look. But, Micah refuses, absolutely refuses, to get back in the wagon and ride to somewhere else. When I suggest we walk, he looks out onto the streets once more and tells me that this place is fine.

The ragged sign hung above the door has something scrawled on it, but it’s become unreadable over the years. The black markings of the letters drip down until all that’s left is a board with a black smear across it. Micah pulls the warped wooden door open with a gentlemanly flourish. “After you.”

I nod my thanks, walking across the threshold and into the tavern. It’s long and skinny, a counter along one side and tables along the other. At the end of the narrow room is a door, leading to the ‘hotel’ part, I guess. Another smeared sign hangs above that door as well. The air is stale, but it’s not the worst we’ve been at of recent.

Dirt stained floorboards creak as I walk down them, taking the stool closest to the door at the end. I feel it’s something Arlan would’ve done for some reason or other. Micah sits on the stool next to me and it creaks underneath his skinny self, threatening to give way.

The Tender is busy with the other patrons at the counter with us, taking orders and filling drinks. Handling money and food. Clearing away used tin plates and copper cups, making his way down the bar top. When he reaches us, the bar is already half full, and nobody is Fearless.

“Can I help you?” somebody asks, and I focus. I was staring intently at the door, willing Fearless to pass through it.

“What?” I blink, giving my head a slight shake. The Tender stands across the counter from me, drying his hands with a flour towel.

"Do you want anything to drink?" he asks again, slinging the towel over his shoulder and positioning both hands on the counter.

I look to Micah, who shrugs at me.

"No," I say to the Tender, "We're fine for right now."

"If you're sure," he says, slowly blinking. The Tender looks at me, shaking his head. "I'm sorry, but have we met before?"

"I don't think so," I tell him, though I hadn't really paid much mind before now. He's tall, broad, with light brown hair and green eyes, and a nose that's crooked enough to suggest it's been broken more than once.

The young Tender nods at this before turning to walk back up the bar. "Wait," I say, tilting my chin, "Connor?"

"Georgia?" he asks, furrowing his brows and stepping closer, a broad smile plastered across his face. "What are you doing here?"

"I could ask you the same question," I say, laughing, leaning across the bar and embracing him. "What happened to Port Seaglass?"

"Money ran out," he says. "But you! You look so different. You look better."

"Aw, Connor," I say, "You look better too. Almost didn't recognize you."

"I'm sorry," Micah says, interjecting, leaning in, "But have you two met before?"

"No," I say, teasing him.

"Let me rephrase," he says, shifting his weight on his elbows. "Where have you met before?"

"Oh, I was just little Georgie's love interest," Connor says, filling a glass with golden ale and handing it to a man behind us.

"No, you were not, and don't call me Georgie," I tell him. I turn to Micah, "He was another drummer, the one Janson replaced."

"Oh, well, that's… that's quite lovely. So, tell me… Connor…" Micah begins, dropping his voice. "Does anyone come to this bar… anyone of importance?"

"Importance," Connor laughs, "This ole river bar? Nah."

Micah looks at the ceiling, waving his hand, searching for words, trying a few false starts before breaking off.

"Connor," I say, nudging Micah and lowering my voice, too. "Fearless Le Paige. Does she come here?"

Connor jerks, eyes wide and filled with fear. His broad hands grab my shoulders as he leans close to whisper, "Why are you looking for her? Don't. Go home, back to the castle, bring your friend with you, and forget it ever happened."

"Connor," I say, looking at him, "I can't." I pause. "Does she come here?"

"I don't know," he says, letting go of my shoulders and straightening up again, composure regained. "Nobody knows what she looks like. She's more of a myth here- a legend…"

"Bar Tender," calls someone down the bar, cutting him off.

"Hold on a minute," Connor shouts back. He takes a deep breath before continuing. "All we know, down here, is that whoever goes looking doesn't come back." He picks up a clean glass from the rack behind him and begins to aggressively polish it, to do something with his hands. I remember that about him.

"Ok," Micah says, finally saying something, "Does a lady come here, dressed in-what? - a blue frock coat, with no sleeves, long brown hair, boots?"

"Yeah," he says, blinking, his green eyes scrunching up. "Every evening. Orders a golden meade and leaves."

"That's her."

"That's Fearless? That lady wouldn't hurt anybody." Connor fills a glass with something, passing it down to a person farther down the bar. "She comes in every night at eight."

Micah pulls out a pocket watch from his vest, flashing the face towards me. Half 'till eight. "What do we do when she gets here?"

"I'll get her meade, same as always," Connor says, polishing the glass harder, "What do you want from her?"

"Well," I say, hesitantly. "Arlan and Micah's brother, Nathan, broke into her house, and she kidnapped them."

Connor's eyes grow wide, a stone-blooded curse floating out on his sigh. "Geez, lass, don't you ever get into any normal trouble? Why do you have to go after a killer?"

"We didn't know where else to go," Micah says, taking a sip from the glass of water that Connor put on the counter. "These fell out the window- I think Arlan dropped these out the window, but we don't know why." He reaches into his pockets, pulling out the lightning-painted sticks and the journal, setting them on the wooden bar counter.

Except that the journal isn't a journal. And not Arlan's journal like we thought.

Stamped into the cover of the journal is a circle, edged in dots, with two swords crossed over each other, offset. "This isn't Arlan's," Micah says, tracing the swords on the cover. "Moreover, it's not vinegar paper." And indeed, it isn't. The paper of the journal in front of us is thick, rich. Expensive. Not thin, like it's brother, carried in Arlan's pocket.

And the binding. Though worn, it was rich, right. The pages, glued into the spine, not bound with cheap thread, like ones drummers can afford. "Does that mean… it belongs to Fearless?" The words stand in the air, like sentry-soldiers.

"One would suppose," Micah says, pushing the threadbare book just a tad further away and setting his hands into his lap.

I reach out and open the cover, revealing words. The words are both printed across the page and scrawled in the margins. The words filled in by Fearless are written with a heavy hand, the spider-y letters spinning over each other. The book that lies in front of us details fighting; hand-to-hand combat, really. The notes written between the lines are on how she fights.

"Invaluable," Connor says, flipping through the pages and drawing a finger across the writing. "Really, it is." The moment that follows is full of something. Suspense, perhaps, but mostly nerves. Connor grabs the book, reading aloud the notes scrawled in the front pages, the binding ones that come between the cover and the first pages of printing.

These pages seem a synopsis of all in the book, detailing her favor of the hammer fist and catch-grab-punch technique. How she manages to avoid her own favored attacks, with a thumb release and a counter-attack.

How all fights are just attack, defense, counter attack.

"How could Fearless keep all of this written down?" Micah asks, rubbing his stubbly jaw with his hand, "It's so foolish!" He opens his mouth to say more, but before he can Connor goes stiff. He stands up straight, picking himself up from his slouched position over the counter.

I turn.

Standing in the doorway is Fearless Le Paige.

Chapter Seventeen

****

I pry my eyes open. Nathan is lying on the floor, not more than an arm's length away. I sit up, my muscles protesting every movement.

"Janson," I say, "Janson?"

"Arlan?" someone says. I turn my head to the left, with much effort. The small muscles in my neck strain, and I see Janson sitting in the lone chair.

"Janson," I say again, my voice hoarse. "What time is it?" The light in the room is dark, the beam that was streaming through the hole in the wall is gone.

"Who knows?" he replies, looking up from the book splayed in his lap. He stands, offering me a cup he pulled from the mantle of the fire place. "How are you feeling?"

"Thrown," I say, trying to convince my arm to take the drink. It finally complies, taking the water and spilling some on the way to my mouth.

"Ah," he says, "But better, though, right?"

"Aye." I take another drink. The water helps, it clears the fog that's in my head. "It must be late," I say, gesturing to the moonbeam coming through the shelves.

"Aye," Janson replies. He stoops low, scooping wood from a firebox I hadn't noticed before.

"What are you doing?"

"Isn't it obvious? Building a fire."

My mind starts putting things together, like the puzzles that young lads and lasses do. Two pieces meet.

"Can you climb up the chimney?"

"Already tried," Janson replies, striking a match against the cold stone of the hearth. "Blocked by iron grates. Bars as thick as your thumb."

I sit back, studying the fireplace. It's set in the same grey stone as the rest of the house is hewn in, with a long, flat piece jutting out for a mantle. Through the back, though, I can see into the other room,

"What about crawling through, into the main room."

Janson builds up the fire in the place now. "Grates. Bars thicker than the others."

“Oh,” I say.

“Look, Arlan, I’ve tried everything to get out. Even tried to pick the lock. It doesn’t work.” The fire has caught now, the orange-red flames leaping to and fro, but never leaving the confines of the stone hearth, not that there’s much to burn on this side.

“Arlan,” Janson says, breaking the silence. “What are you going to do? Now that you’re here?”

I hesitate. Janson rocks back on his heels. “She’s not here- left for town a quarter ago. She’s always out long at evetime.”

“Wait,” I say, by means of formulated plan. “Stay and wait to be rescued.”

“Rescued? By who?”

“Georgia and Micah,” I say. Nathan stirs across the small, stone room, running his hand along his jaw and sitting up.

“But you said that Georgia’s not here,” Janson insists, slipping from the chair to the ground, to be eye level with me.

“She’s here,” I say, taking another sip. “She came.”

“Really?” Janson asks, again. He leans forward on his knees, a smile across his face.

“Aye,” I say, stressing the syllable. “But, what about you. Tell us what happened since I last saw you.”

"I woke up when I was grabbed from behind," he says, taking the cup from me and drinking from it. "The person- Fearless- stuffed my head in some kind of bag and drug me to the cart."

"Why didn't you scream?" I ask, not even caring that I interrupted.

"I couldn't," he says. "She choked me. I couldn't get enough air into my lungs to scream."

"And then?"

"And then I was here and here I've been, miserable and starving. Until you came," Janson says. He folds the book's page down, to mark his place, and puts on the mantle, next to the cup and a few empty jars.

"What about Fearless?" This is Nathan. He's standing, peering out the bookshelf window.

"What about her?" Janson asks.

"Why did she kidnap you?"

"I don't know," Janson tells him, "She keeps asking about papers, and fires, but I don't know what she's talking about."

"Papers and fires?"

"More specifically, papers burnt in fires. More than that, the fire that my parents perished in." This seems to come out in a rush, like the floodgate has been broken and not opened. Open has control, broken doesn't.

"What do you mean, papers?"

"Government papers, papers that I don't know about. Spy papers, history, language, I don't know, papers she's convinced I read." His voice gets louder with every word, with every 'I don't know.'

"Did you read them?"

"No," Janson says, his voice crescendoing to a point. "I try to keep telling her that, but she won't listen to me." He's up now, and moving around. He walks to the far corner of the room and back again, pacing lines in the floor.

"Great, you broke him," Nathan says, standing and stilling Janson, one great hand on each of the boy's shoulders.

"I'm… I'm well," Janson says, face marked with worry, sitting back down in the chair and putting the book back in his lap, where it probably won't get read.

"What are you reading?" I ask him, peering over his shoulder at the yellowing pages.

"O'Connor."

****

The lady comes around, draping herself in the chair next to Micah.

"Your meade, lass," Connor says, sliding the frosted glass across the worn counter.

"I'm a lot older than a lass, lad," she says, her voice low. She smiles, her eyes all squinty. She's a lot more wrinkled that I would have thought, wrinkles spread across taught cheeks and away from sharp, blue eyes.

"My mistake," Connor says, barely paying attention to her smile. He vigorously polishes a glass; I'm sure it's going to give and break, shattering across the floor. Fearless polishes off the drink, pushing the glass towards the center of the counter.

"Another?" asks Connor, taking the glass and putting it in the wrought iron sink behind him.

"Another?" She echoes, mockingly, "Do I ever have another?"

"I just thought…" Connor says, trailing off and staring off, resuming his furious polishing.

"No, not another," Fearless says, exasperatedly. "Never another. One drink is fine, always fine, any more and you border on drunk. Here's your silver." She plunks a silver coin on the counter, and it rolls right towards Connor before stopping, dangerously close to the edge. He picks up the coin, slipping it in the breast pocket of his buttoned blue shirt.

I dig my elbow in Micah's ribs, and he shifts. "Not even if that drink cost naught?" he asks, somewhat pained, to Fearless. Then, his face shifts, and his voice gets lower and smoother. Like a stage act that got switched on. Micah nods at Connor, who fills up another glass and slides it across the counter to him.

"Here," Micah says, offering the glass to Fearless.

"Oh, well, I appreciate it much, but I've got appointments," Fearless says, stepping off the stool.

"No, now I really must insist," Micah says, holding the glass out to her and winking. She hesitates a moment, taking it and drinking a bit off the top.

"If you insist," she says, sitting back down. "I'm not one to waste good alcohol, especially alcohol already poured."

"This?" Micah says, "This, good alcohol?"

"Aye."

"This is not good," Micah says, "This is barely alcohol. Tender." He turns to Connor and raises a glass, "Get this fine lady my usual."

"Aye," Connor says, moving to get a glass.

"Something strong," I say, turning away from Micah and Fearless and covering all but the corner of my mouth with my hand, "Very strong." He nods, pouring some cocktails together, topping it with a dash of green powder.

He hands it to Micah, who is watching Fearless drain the last few drips of her golden meade. "Thank you."

"What was that?" I ask Connor as Fearless swallows the small glass of alcohol in one gulp. She coughs, hard, leaning over.

"Something I mix up when sailors come in and want to lose the light of day," he responds, crossing his arms over his stomach and watch her. "With a little bit of mountain powder mixed in to hasten it."

"Mountain powder?"

"Hastens the alcohol. Gets her out fast," Connor explains.

Mountain powder and it's many uses saves us again. It is now that I doubt there's anything that chemical can't do.

Over on the counter, Fearless is tracing her fingers around the rim of the small glass, her head collapsed on her arms. She is talking, but it's not making any sense. "…and I really must be going," Micah was saying.

Fearless nods, her head dropping lower as it lolls from side to side. She starts to get up, and it's a bit like watching a babe learn how to walk. Her body moves but her head stays still. When it finally catches up, it throws her off and into the arms of Connor, who had moved behind her.

"Madam, I really insist that you not go out," he says, trying to right her and realizing that her legs can't take weight.

"I must." She struggles, either out of his arms or onto her feet, it's hard to tell.

"Madam, let me get you a room. There are spares above the bar."

"What?" she asks as he grabs a key from the wall, ushering her through the door at the end of the room. I see him tilt his head back and turn, nodding at us as we trip over the threshold of the door and out into the night.

****

The silence is almost overbearing. Every breath that I hear sounds like a cannon blast into the night. I can hear every breath, every blink. There is no sound. Even in the middle of the Dire Forest, we had music. Music Micah would play on his stringed instruments, just to pass the time. But this torture, this is…

"What was that?" I ask, standing. It was a thump, on the door. Or, more possibly, it's just me, going crazy.

"I don't know," Janson says, standing up. We crowd around the door to the main room, vying for the ability to peer out the window. The door knob is turning slowly, the brazen knob to the main door. It opens and a cloaked figure steps inside. It- she- turns, letting the moonbeam wash over her face.

"Georgia!" I call, softly. It startles her, and she jumps and turns, hand at her waist, where I know she has a knife hidden between the layers of her skirt.

"It's Janson!" Janson says, pushing me out of the way. "Georgia."

"Where are you!?"

"Over here."

"Where's here?" She turns in circles, surveying the damage of the fight and scanning the walls. Finally, she sees us, coming over to the shelf, shoving her face to the hole in the wall and sticking her fingers through the bars, where they touch Janson's. A scream of joy threatens to spill over the carefully constructed barricade of silence, but it doesn't.

She takes a deep breath and scoots back from the wall. "Is this the lock?" she asks. I nod, but she bends down and examines it.

"Is there a key?"

"Aye," Janson says, shoving me out of the way again. "It's around Fearless's neck."

"Well, there's no Fearless, and no key," Georgia says, frustratingly throwing the lock against the door. It hits the wood with a thump and nothing else.

Another taller, cloaked figure moves towards Georgia, the long, lanky walk of Micah. “Can you pick it?” he asks, bending down next to her.

“No,” Georgia says, picking up the lock once more, “I don’t know how to pick locks.”

“Of all your miscellaneous skills, picking locks isn’t among them?”

“No,” she says, frustrated, throwing it against the wall again, hoping anger will break it.

“Never mind this,” Nathan says, shoving me and Janson out of the way, “what did you do with Fearless?”

“Certainly not enough,” a chilling voice answers from the corner. We all turn in horror to see Fearless Le Paige standing in the doorway, hand on either hip, cloak flowing majestically in the wind.

Chapter Eighteen

"But..." Micah struggles to get out, "but..."

"What about the alcohol?" she asks, laughing and straightening the front of her sleeveless deep blue frock coat. "That was mountain powder in it, right? Mountain powder to speed up the drunkenness?"

A dumbfounded Georgia nods.

"It also speeds up the hangover," she whispers, "That and my special cure... more mountain powder."

For a long second, nobody moves.

And then a knife flies out of nowhere and embeds itself in the wall next to Fearless's right shoulder. Georgia stands, poised, the glint of the knife at her waist gone. "My dear," Fearless says, leaning her shoulder against the flat of the embedded dagger, her feet crossed at the ankles, "Though I do applaud your valor, you're going to have to try much harder than that…" But she doesn't get farther in her speech when Georgia step-punches her in the throat, throwing Fearless's back against the wall.

A startled gasp escapes my lips, and Georgia steps back, staring at her hands in disbelief. But, Fearless recovers far too quickly, already reaching to grab Micah, who's nearer. As soon as her fingers wrap around his boney wrist, he pulls to the thumb and narrowly avoids the fist that flies towards his face, instead leaning out and striking her hard one across the cheek.

It's a loud hit, and it'll bruise, for sure. But she expects it and rolls with the force, throwing her leg out and sweeping Micah's from under him. He falls and lands on his back and…

Nathan pushes me off the side and begins throwing his weight against the door in the wall, desperate to get in and to help. I help with the next heave, and my shoulder throbs with the force. But the door doesn't give. We hear more punches and thumps as the fight rages on in the next room, and the force of not being able to fight fuels us as we batter the door and our shoulders. Stuff falls from the shelves, padding the floor with books and broken tchotchkes, I hear them falling. And I throw myself against that wall, over and over again.

I need to get in there, I need to help. I need to get in there, I need to help. I have to help. I must help.

I hit the door again, with every bit of strength and weight I have.

But the door doesn't budge.

****

The bookshelf door starts to tremble suddenly as Arlan and the others begin to throw themselves against it, trying to break out. The shelves begin to fall, and the air is filled with their war cries.

"Micah," I gasp, suddenly, my hair being violently pulled from my head. I try to grab her hands, wrapped in my locks, trying to pry it loose or something, but… I kick blindly behind me, trying to get purchase, to no avail. A sharp pain in my side, my collar bone burns with a hammer fist I didn't give, then…

The hand lets go of my hair.

Micah's picked up Fearless around the waist, pinning her arms down at her sides. I grab the chain around her neck, pulling at the brazen key. The chain digs into the skin of her neck, the thick metal refusing to give. But I just pull harder, a quick yank to snap the chain and she screams, partly in rage and part in pain.

Micah restrains Fearless as I struggle my way across the floor, to free those trapped in the room, but I hear a sickening crunch as Micah falls to the ground and Fearless rushes towards me. The lock pulls down as I'm wrenched away from the door, thrown across the room and into the dark shape of furniture, obscured by the moonlight and warped mountain-powder shadows. As my elbows hit floor and pain explodes through my arm, I roll away from whatever I hit and into the center of the room.

And when my vision clears, there's a knife at my throat.

****

My ears are ringing from all the screaming, the sounds of the fight. But, just as we prepare to run into the door a final time, it opens and we stumble into the main room, our feet just barely below us. Just in time to see Fearless with a blade at Georgia's throat.

And I can't think.

****

"Make another move, and the girl dies," the notorious Fearless Le Paige says, holding a knife to my throat. My knife. I am my own demise. Her knee is on my chest, my arms underneath me. Just as my knife restricts my life, my body restricts my freedom.

"Just put it down," Nathan says from across the room, hauling himself to his feet, "The knife. No one has to die now."

"You think I'll just let you all walk away with my informant?" Fearless says, "I need those papers that he read."

"That was four years ago!" Janson screams, "I didn't read them!"

The knife edge is pressed a little harder against my throat, a hard line, surely drawing blood.

"No?" she asks, and I see something click behind her eyes like clock gears.

"I didn't, I swear!" Janson shouts, showing his palms in sincerity. "I swear!"

The knife draws blood, and I daren't breathe.

****

"Alright," Fearless says, removing the knife and tucking it into the sidestrap of her boot, "I believe you."

"What?" Micah asks in disbelief.

"I believe you. If your country goes to war, that's not my problem, not anymore," she says, bluntly. "And you better thank whatever God you pray to that you're such good fighters, worthy adversaries, or else I wouldn't let you go."

Let us go?

She continues, snarling, "It's not like anyone's going to believe your story, anyway."

And with that, she stands and runs out the open door, jumping onto the canyon at full speed.

There's a moment where no one moves, and pain doesn't exist. My shoulders don't ache with the force of the weight they've been under, my face doesn't burn, the first time in seemingly days. There's no feeling, just numbness that fades into disbelief. Nathan staggers to the door, looking down into the watery gorge and shakes his head in astonishment.

"Did she ever really exist?" I ask, pulling myself up looking around and down the quarry anyway, but there's nothing. No blood on rocks, no figure swimming away, running away. She disappeared into thin air.

"I guess it all fits, I suppose," Georgia says, still shaken from all that's happened. She draws her hand to her throat, where a thin line of blood has begun running into the hem of her dress. Then, Georgia's purple eyes glaze over and she begins to fall, her limbs folding in on herself. Arms outstretched, I catch her waist before she hits the ground, brushing a strand of her dark hair from her face and lowering her to the ground, as gently as I could.

And we start walking toward the wagon, shell shocked, at a loss for words.

****

Epilogue

I don't remember ever leaving Fearless's cave. I don't remember how the fight ended, and I don't believe Arlan when he told me. Fearless just, disappear into thin air, like that? It sounds more like myth than reality, but to tell truth, so does most of our story. There are still parts I don't know. They told me I fainted and Arlan carried me out of there, to the wagon, where Ole Amos carried me back to Alyak and to the inn where Connor worked. And there we spent the night.

When I look back at all that had happened, it seems unreal. Fearless left with the warning that nobody would ever believe our story, and sometimes I don't either. The words recorded in Arlan's journal should be published as some type of children's story, some type of storybook, something that should end with us being received as heroes and nothing else.

But, Arlan was received as a kidnapper, I as kidnapped, and Janson as a runaway. Or, at least, that's what most of the kingdom believes. That's what ran in the paper and was spread on the over-crowded street corners of the cities. The handprint scar on Arlan's face, red and textured more like leather than skin, it meant naught. No show of our harrowing journey. All it means is that he can't be a Drummer anymore, and that he was sent out, not even paid like one retired. Banished, or something like it.

Arlan went back to that day-town, the first one, to play with Rosalind and Loren, back at the first day-town. Nathan and Micah play with them sometimes, when they aren't here in Jade City, playing for royal balls and such. Their music has grown in popularity, the Clay Curry Band Wagon is received with such grandeur, you'd think they were royalty. They were certainly received with more welcome than I when I came home.

When I returned home, Mother and Father didn't believe I set out to rescue Janson and chose to believe I ran off with Arlan instead. They took this to mean I shouldn't be wed. I haven't bothered to correct them yet. Maybe I will run away. Who knows?

And the only thing I took away from this harrowing adventure is that, I guess storybook endings are just that:

storybook endings. Endings that only happen in books. The books Arlan reads and writes now, the books that sit untouched in the library now that he's no longer here to read them. They still don't dust in there. I don't let them.

****

They say that everyone gets an adventure in life. I guess this was mine. And I've learned that not everything ends up like a fairy-tale, although it may start like one. "Once upon a time," doesn't always end with "Happily Ever After."

Sometimes, it ends with, "And then they survived."

Acknowledgements

I know that most people don't read the acknowledgements in the back of books, and I am no different. And you don't have to either, but this is where the nitty-gritty happens. This is where I personally thank everyone that goes into a the making of a book. And, I know that most people don't really think that all the people listed in the acknowledgements helped in its writing, at least not significantly, but that's false. If even one of the people below didn't do as fantastic of a job as they did, this book would not have been written. Honestly. I am truly, truly thankful to the people who helped me write this book because, frankly, I'm a mess.

Firstly, to Samuel Elder, whose titles precede him: Chief of Psychology, Research, and Remembrance; and also Head Idea-bouncer. I truly believe this book would not be in existence if it weren't for you and your constant on-call idea bouncing and your ability to name fictional coffee shops and character middle names as fast as you do. From the bottom of my heart, thank you so much.

Secondly, Jacob Gearon and Lani Bergatin, for their constant reading of my work to check for cohesiveness, and whether or not many, many statements really sounded as awkward as I thought they did. Thank you. Collectively, they are responsible for half of the character tags in this book, because I have a tendency to forget that readers can't read my mind, and that I do actually need to include them. An umbrella thank you to Samuel, Jacob, and Lani for keeping me entertained during late nights of editing with all the nonsensical discussions going on in the group-chats.

I would like to thank my mother.

Of course.

But honest and true, my mother is fantastic and has helped me so much with my book and the development of BekahHaasbooks that I can hardly believe it. She has endured my rambling about my books and plotlines and was even there when 7th Drummer wasn't really a book yet, just an idea. Thanks, Mom.

Also, Anna, my faithful sister, who was banging on my wall at 3 am when I was editing this book in the home stretch, yelling at me to go to sleep because she could see the light through the door that connects our two rooms.

Thank you to Elizabeth Downs, who was the last person to beta-read this work, and whose input was very much appreciated. Thank you to everyone who lent parts to the costume picture on the front, and to my brother, Josh, for posing. Thank you, Dad, for making the drum on the cover.

And, to be honest, I don't even play the drums, I play clarinet. So, finally, I would like to thank Ethan Stinehart and Kenny Lockhart, who helped me with everything drum-related. Thank you, Ethan, for lending me your beginner percussion book, and thank you, Kenny, for giving me a copy of last year's marching music and answering stupid questions, like whether or not wearing a bass drum sideways, like a marching snare, would actually kill you. (The answer is yes, it would.)

About the Author

Rebekah Haas started writing at a very young age, and subsequently published her first novel, Scarlet City, at fifteen. This is her second novel and is heavily influenced by her love of music. When she is not writing, she can be found doing homework or practicing her clarinet. She also enjoys reading novels, when she can, and traveling.

Stay updated!

Facebook:
Rebekah Haas

Twitter:
@BekahHaasBooks

Goodreads/ Blog:
Rebekah Haas

If you liked this book, or even if you didn't, please leave a review on Amazon or Goodreads. Thank you so very much!

~Rebekah Haas